Kept

Camille Lindstrom

CAMILLE LINDSTROM

First Edition, 2016

ISBN: 978-1537324326

ACKNOWLEDGMENTS

I am indebted to the following folks for understanding my hibernation and obsession in the production of my first book:

To A.V. Scott, for being an immense help in helping me navigate the publishing world.

To my mom, for believing in me.

To my own tenacity, for kicking me in the ass to finally bring this to fruition.

For all the Do Nothing Bitches. I hope you find what sets
your soul on fire

1

I brush on one final stroke of charcoal shadow.
You couldn't go wrong with the smoky eye, intriguing in
its sultry demeanor. Standing there before the full-
length mirror, I check myself before I go on. My cheeks
aglow with a hint of peach and my athletic 5'7" frame
dressed in my favorite purple number tonight, I feel
sexy. My loose, auburn tendrils fall in a tousled cascade,
evoking a kind of mermaid sex appeal. Smacking on one
last coat of nude lip stain, I'm ready. "Meadow, first
call." Trotting down the stage in my seven inch heels,
the drown of the music begins and squalls of men fidget
in their seats. All eyes are on me.

It's the Marble 500, a prized time for all of us. One
week in February, the streets of Marble Beach, Florida
crawl with hungry race fans. Grocery parking lots
become makeshift tailgating compounds. There's a kind

6

of fiscal jumpstart that infuses everything from restaurants to retailers to hotels. This is the most coveted event of the year to work, and for many of us, the most lucrative.

The club is transformed into a throbbing cache of lust, brimming with men toting a plethora of pursuits—companionship, conversation, a quick sexual thrill, a particular fetish—or the proverbial escape from the nagging wife back home. I always admired the intoxicating energy that filled the club during the 500. The music, pounding into a hypnotizing sensation that pulsated within the onlookers, narrates the sultry shadows of the gyrating female form. Buxom breasts, toned abdominals, legs adorned in stockings—all insignias of seduction. A trail of sweat rolls down my spine, glimmering under the neon spectrum of lights that bounce from wall to wall. I sashay across the stage topless to "My own summer " by the Deftones, looking down at each man perched at the edge with a ubiquitous gaze—eyes big as golf balls, mouth partially open clenching some dollars—their eyes tear into my body, hungry to lap up a cocktail of seduction.

This was the Marble 500 after all. The money was a little different than any other week of the year. As with any event, there was an influx of girls migrating from Miami and the Keys to beyond state lines like Vegas, Nashville and Columbus. On average, we'd hire an average of 160 plus girls a night, in addition to accommodating over a 1,000 customers. We regularly violated the fire code. The club's three bars were fully staffed to four bartenders in addition to bustling bar backs and waitresses who were stretched thin. It was easy to get overwhelmed in there between the crowd, the smoke, and the blaring music.

Marble Beach is a seasonal town, making money unpredictable. It's relatively quiet until the months of January through April, as these are our event months. The Rolex race marks the start of a new race season, always held at the end of January, followed by the Marble 500 in February. After that comes Bike Week in all its leathery glory in March, ultimately being trailed by the yearly pilgrimage of tanned, party seeking collegiate youths: Spring Break. During the 500, a girl could easily pull a minimum of $300-1,000 in a single night; you'd be stupid not to work. Most of us stuck it out to the end of the week, milking what we could out of the race crowd, pulling six or more nights straight. By the end of the week many of us were nursing bruised knees, pulled biceps, and strained vocal cords. Battle wounds of the game.

This Marble 500 would be my fourth one in a row, having been at Posh for four years now, marking my longest running employment streak at a strip club. I never lasted much longer than eight or nine months. Not because of tension but because I seemingly always got tired of the familiar wallpaper and velour couches, and didn't really have a warm and inviting camaraderie with a lot of the dancers. It was more of a dry, civil greeting with an obligatory smile, each conversation opening with, "So, what brings you here?"

At Posh, more of a tight knit bond stood among the house girls. A house girl was defined as a girl who had been there a minimum of one year or longer. For a long time, the only interaction I got with the other girls was on that brass pole—never outside the walls of the club. And while this standoffish attitude predisposed many to misunderstanding me, my driving motivation for doing so was because I didn't have anything in common with the girls. Drugs dominated some of the their lives. Others had a wealthy scroll of ill-fated, toxic relationships, usually with some boyfriend that they supported. At twenty-six, my lips had never touched a cigarette, I couldn't discern baby powder from cocaine, and I had no clue how to roll a marijuana blunt. As far as I was concerned, it transformed people into languid couch potatoes, transfixed with an innocuous spot on the wall. Someone like me was the minority. Instead of bags of Roxicets or cocaine, I had envelopes labeled for goals. I shopped with tennis moms at Trader Joe's. I opted for a good sweat session in the gym as opposed to sitting around getting high all day.

Of the constant nomadic population of dancers there, I had only one friend with whom I hung out with outside work. And even that had taken a few years to happen. Sarah and I were of the minority—that is, dancers who weren't jaded by freeloading boyfriends, drug meddling, or a myriad of dysfunction.

Sarah was a reserved but friendly girl whom I admired from afar for a long time. When she took the stage the chaotic energy of the club went into slow motion. Her languid movements exuded a palpable sensuality to the breathy chords of Sade, sedating every man in her gaze. Curvy with bronzed, supple skin and doe eyes that had a disarming quality, she possessed a patience that I admired, especially on particularly slow nights; she always kept her presence of mind. I was the one who too often got frustrated.

Our work was highly stigmatized and misunderstood. As a result, many of us kept our lucrative income a secret from our families and immediate people in our lives. It has been dubbed as sex work, inherently degrading and an easy way out. Any woman who chose to dance half naked for leering strangers surely had no self-respect or dignity. But I didn't see it that way. I saw it as the one industry where women made more than men, where manipulation and charm came together to squeeze every last dollar out of some pathetic man paying for someone's attention. A lot it came down to entertaining fantasies that ultimately would never happen, leaving the guys to go back home and take care of their sorry selves. But they weren't all pathetic. We had businessmen, young twentysomethings who sat with their arms glued to their sides during their very first lap dance, bachelor parties and lonely men who needed to feel wanted, even desired. These were the easiest ones to make money off of. To me, it was a power rush, a form of mild misandry in lingerie. The men were like sitting ducks. You knew the drill: bat your lashes. Smile. Appear interested in the conversation. Find common ground. Don't sit any longer than twenty minutes. Close the sale. Onto the next victim.

* * *

After straining our vocal chords the previous five hours over the drown of music, the drive home was often the one thing I looked forward to the most; the placid silence, the salt-tinged breeze filtering in from the ocean, whipping my hair about, giving consolation to my tired body. In that small world of women where we shared that smoky neon haze until 2:30 A.M., there were a few cardinal rules:

1.) Don't step on toes.

2.) Don't disrespect a house girl.

3.) Hold on to a good, loyal customer like gold.

The third rule was always in heavy pursuit because there were many advantages to having a regular. On slow nights with a thin crowd, a regular could be the answer to financial woes, guaranteeing some security within an otherwise dismal night. But with regulars a girl had to proceed with caution. Sometimes there stood a nonverbal air of reciprocation. Regulars always had a shelf life. Eventually, they got tired of going home with blue balls. They all wanted more than what you were willing to give. There were countless invitations to dinners, parties or hotels. If one could find a customer who offered these things but didn't expect something more as a payout, then one was on their way to something truly rare and special.

2

The tap on my shoulder was cold to the touch. I wipe a bead of sweat from my brow, exiting the stage. A pair of icy, stoic eyes looked down to me as I turned around.

"That was pretty impressive up there. Won't you sit down and join us?"

He was dark. Captivating. Mercurial. Terribly tall. I presumed late thirties. Thirty-seven?

"Well I—I," stammering, I couldn't find my words. "I had a dance to do over there at that table, I'll be over after."

Shoving a $100 into my hand, he glints at me.

"No, won't you sit down? Would you like a drink?"

Well Jesus Christ I guess I should then. Motioning for me to come to his table, an ice bucket of beers sat on it.

With the Marble 500, the object was to move from table to table in an effort to make the most money. You didn't make any money being idle—unless of course, you got lucky with a lucrative table. In that case, you didn't have to move anywhere.

"I don't usually drink much at work. Like to stay focused."

"Ah, no worries. So what do you want?"

Okay so he's blatantly ignoring me. *What the hell, what's one beer?*

"I'll have a Heineken, thanks."

"So what's your name?"

"Meadow." As a rule, we never revealed our real names. Partially for security and anonymity.

"Nice to meet you. I'm Jack. And this is Tim." Pointing to his comrade a few tables over, he looked slightly older than Jack by about ten years. Arms languidly cast aside like some limp puppet, he was immersed in a drunken robotic rendition of a lap dance. Some of the girls couldn't do the job without numbing their senses.

"Cool. You guys here for the race?"

"Yeah, we come down every year for it."

"Where are you guys from?"

"Marsh Harbor."

With Marsh Harbor being about an hour and a half stretch north, presumably what these guys were seeking was also some anonymity.

"So you wanna do some dances?" Jack asked, winking at me.

I was put off by his hasty desire to get in the back room. But I also didn't mind it either. Sometimes it was quite the opposite, with guys throwing every excuse in the book as to why they didn't want a dance. I need more drinks. My girlfriend is here. I promised my wife no dances. I ran out of money. All of these various euphemisms for being a broke-ass.

Posh offered two types of dances. Ones on the floor went for $10, sans contact. Ones in the back room were $20, involved above the waist contact and were carried out in tiny rooms similar to that of an office cubical. Dimly lit, they ensured a more intimate setting.

We take a seat in the back and Jack's desires spring to life. Straddling him, I remove my bra. My hair spills over my bare breasts as I gyrate back and forth, rubbing my knee in his crotch. A hardening begins to emerge. Starting with his temples, I draw a trail with my fingers over the crescent of his stubbly cheeks and bloated belly, finishing over his khaki shorts. Planting minute kisses on his hands, I feel the cold of his wedding band, but that didn't mean anything. Most of the guys were married. Why they were here? Countless reasons. A fantasy in which the wife cannot—or will not fulfill. Marital discord. Vice. Or perhaps a thirsty philanderer that can't keep it in his pants.

Many of the guys hid this side from their wives, adopting a kind of compartmentalization. We saw the man many wives would never see—the repressed, carnal spirit that had been surrendered the day they walked down the aisle. Marital vows that seemingly went on hiatus the moment they walked through our doors. Morals—or anything remotely close— were replaced by uninhibited requests that were easily delivered with the help of alcohol. I could write a book on the drunken requests and newfound confidence these guys came at me with. It was enough to make any woman a misanthrope of the opposite sex.

"Eye contact." Jack mutters demandingly. His formidable pretense put my nerves on edge, but I kept my brown eyes with his blue ones. They were beautiful, but with a kind of emptiness that had me curious as to why he was here other than the race. By the fifth dance, tiny beads of sweat formed a trail down the nape of my neck. Nestling my face into the nook of his neck and shoulder, I sucked on his earlobe and exhaled into his ear, rhythmically moving my pelvis back and forth.

"You broke a sweat, huh?" He says breathlessly, his hands on my back, pushing me into him.

The hardening was more intense now, that's how you knew you were giving a successful dance. I changed to reverse cowgirl, my hair whipping him in the face. Taking a handful, he tugs my head back as I go on for another ten songs. We finally exit the back room. Sore and dank, I try to mask a mild limp. I'd done a total of fifteen songs. $300. And it was only 10:30.

We go back to the table and I slump down in my chair, holding my hair up as I fan my face.

"Another beer?" Jack asks.

"No, I think I'm good." I pick at a newly minted rash near my panty line from the fifteen songs I'd just pulled. Must have been the belt buckle.

Sitting there with him, I ask a common icebreaker.

"So what do you do?"

"You mean, for work?" Tilting a Heineken back, Jack's eyebrows shot up.

"That would be it."

"Uh, real estate."

Well that's a rather vague delivery. My head searched for variables. Commercial? Residential? Before I can elaborate deeper he shifts the spotlight to me.

"And what about you? Is this all you do?"

I hated this question, especially right now as I currently floundered to find my path. It was a transitional period in academia for me. I had been studying phlebotomy for the past year and a half, and while it was interesting, a recent revelation had shown me that I wasn't right for the field.

"No. Well, I was in school for phlebotomy..."

A puzzled look runs across his face as I trail off.

"The people who draw blood. But then I found I get queasy at the sight of blood. I had gone into it for the demand, not the passion. Now I'm trying to figure out what's next. I do like to write."

"Well it's important you pursue where your talent lies. Whatever your talent is, go for that. The hard part is finding a way to make a living off it. A lot of people go to work everyday miserable as hell."

He rolls his eyes and I wonder if that is an implicit reference to himself. An awkward silence overtakes our table as squalls of people decked out in checkered racing apparel continue to fill the club.

"You wanna go back again? You cooled off?" He wasted no time.

My last gulp of beer rolling down my throat, I stood up.

"Sure. Yeah, let's go," Nodding obligingly, we go back for round two. Round two turned into three and four and so on, to the point where I lost count of exactly how many dances I had done. They were all for Jack. I never left his side. He never *let* me leave his side. But then again, I didn't really want to; he was the most interesting man I'd met that night and also the most lucrative customer.

Camille Lindstrom

3

2:00 A.M. Where had the night gone? Counting the money, I stuff $1,100 into my wallet along with one simple request: to make a phone call on my way home. On the underside of a business card read a phone number and a short message: "Call me. Jack."

I cruise down the lonely orange glow of A1A, the ocean in a lull off to my left. The best part of the night was driving home. To be out of those clunky heels, to feel the salt-tinged breeze hitting my face, was a nice respite from the nicotine haze I had just spent the past five hours in.

Drunks stagger back and forth on the sidewalk. The homeless ravage the trashcans. Cars full of alcohol-fueled kids dangle out the windows. The occasional prostitute trots down the corner. Fifteen minutes later I arrive home, a first floor one bedroom. Nothing too fancy but it worked for me, and it was in a gated community. I light a candle and the scent of bamboo fills the air as I undress. An incessant need to get clean prevented me from rarely hitting the sack before showering. A billow of steam envelops me as I outstretch my tired limbs on the bottom of the tub, the trickle of hot water causes me to nod off and then wake again.

I drop the towel and look at the business card on my armoire. I'd always held a vehement stance against girls carousing with customers. Over the years I had rained on many hopeful parades, firing back with remarks pregnant with sass.

"I'll pay you to go to dinner with me."

If there were a price, you could never afford it.

"I'm staying at the Hilton, room 205."

Really? That's great. Enjoy your stay.

"I'll give you anything; a car, shopping sprees, you can even take a ride on my yacht down in Naples."

No thanks. I've already got a brand new car—in full working condition.

"What are you doing later?"

Going home—to my pillow.

"Well that's one lucky pillow."

Sigh...

Reminiscing on these ridiculous requests, it
brought me back to Jack, whom I'd just made over
$1,000 off of tonight. Despite his hefty tab he hadn't
come at me with any of the aforementioned remarks;
there was an air of class about him that had me frozen in
the middle of my bedroom at nearly 4:00 A.M., a moral
tug-of-war about whether to call him riddling my moral
compass.

Why was I so preoccupied about a guy whom I'd
just met? And a customer at that? Why wasn't he falling
into the category of others? Staring blankly at the card,
the numbers throb at me. I pick up the phone. I cancel
the call. I pick up the phone again. And this time I dial.

"Hello?" A deep, frank voice greets me on the other end.

"Hi—uh, it's Meadow. From the—"

"Posh. Yes. Had a fun night tonight. So what's your real
name?" Wow. Was I dealing with a type A personality
or what? He liked to interject. I was still using my stage
name; why I didn't know. Habit, I guess.

"Yes. I mean, it was crazy in there, but that's to be

expected during the races. Always overwhelming. My real name is Lara by the way. So are you driving home?"

"Yeah, long drive back."

And then the dreaded few seconds of awkward silence set in. *What to say, what to say?* My thoughts go haywire and I struggle to offer something to the colloquial drawing board that I was sharing at what was now, 4:15 A.M.

"So do you travel much?"

"Yes, I love to travel. Been to Europe twice."

"Really?" His voice shoots up through the phone. "Now that's impressive. Where did you go?"

"Norway and most recently, just got back from ten days in Switzerland. I have some friends in Zurich. It was beautiful, I didn't want to leave."

"Wow. I was in Italy a few years ago and London a few years before that for work."

"You know it's funny because when I came back, a lot of the girls were in awe that I actually went abroad. I told them it's not that hard, you just have to save your money."

"Very true."

The man was surprisingly easy to talk to. That formidable pretense I'd captured earlier in the night had seemed to fade.

"Well most of them are probably spending their money on other things. Things that won't benefit them, like the memories you'll hold onto from your travels."

He had a point. I'd seen girls make $500 in a night and be broke by the following day.

"What I do every year after the races and Bike Week have passed is put some money aside for a trip. It's my treat to myself after dealing with the madness. I do that and also frequent the beach."

"Frequent?"

Was he mocking me?

"Yes. As in, go to often."

He scoffs through the phone. "I know what frequent means, go on."

"After dealing with the crowd night after night, the last thing I want to do is be near any civilization. So I take myself to the beach, just get lost in the waves."

"Anyone come with you?"

"No, I like my solitude. I think it's inherent to anyone's quality of life. You've got to have time to yourself."

"True. Well, I should let you go. I'm just about home. It was nice talking with you. Thanks for calling. I enjoyed tonight. Talk to you later."

Hanging up, I analyze his last words. *Talk to me later? Would there be a later? He was already assuming there would be a later?*

* * *

I pour the coffee and rub the sleep from my eyes. I study the swirl of the cream, indicative of my thoughts that were on a spin since last night. I didn't have any high hopes of the conversation I had had last night. Jack would probably fall into that category of others, coming at me with an unwanted slew of invitations and bribes laced with sexual innuendoes.

A few weeks later…

My days had become inundated with texts and phone calls. Jack had gotten acquainted with my early evening beach jogs as he called most often on his drive home from work. In fact, that's what I was doing now; sitting on the beach, phone attached to ear with the occasional sand flick to the face. The winds were fierce today.

"So does your wife know when you skip off to the strip club?"

Jack lets out a chuckle. "Definitely not. I keep a backup T-shirt in the car to change into before going home."

Damn. A professional.

I presumed Jack was under that cloud of monotony that hit some marriages. Maybe he was unhappy. Maybe he wasn't. Maybe he just needed some stimulation. A thrill. A taste of danger. It wasn't a far off assertion to make that our male patrons were gamblers—bidding for attention that could be bought. This led me to wonder why men even got married. If they couldn't keep true to the vows they'd taken and resorted to a life of chicanery, what the hell was the point? My mind became a receptacle of questions that went unanswered. Why was this man so interested in me? Why did he care? Who was he? What did he want? Maybe he didn't want anything. Maybe I was a victim of my own circumstance.

Before I could get deeper, he switched the subject.

"So what do you think about dinner Wednesday?"

Dinner? What does he mean dinner? As in, me, him, and a big wide table between to better separate us should he try any vulgarities? Oh no. This was against everything I stood for. I couldn't go. He'd probably cap the night off by asking me to come meet him at a hotel or something. I really didn't want him to be *that* guy; like the others.

"Uh, I don't know. I might have something going on that day."

"Okay. What about Thursday?"

Man, he was persistent.

My voice hung frozen on the line. He wasted no time. I tripped over some dubious words.

"Possibly. Maybe."

"Okay. Well just to let you know, I've got an envelope here at my desk with about $400 with your name on it."

My eyebrows furrowing, I clear my voice.

"Four hundred dollars? For what?"

"Well I figure you won't be going to work that night so I wanted to make sure you were compensated for your time."

"Okay, let me call you back in a few minutes."

Seriously? For dinner? I stood there, frozen on the beach as the gusts whipped my hair in my face, attempting to shake me into reality while I contemplated his businesslike tenor. I didn't know how to navigate it. I'd never been in this situation before. I called the only person whom I thought could help: Sarah.

4

March 2011

"Just tell him you'll go to dinner, but that I'm going to tag along."

Sarah had had an onslaught of regulars over the years. Some local, some from beyond state lines. And so I thought any advice she could lend would be helpful.

The thought of her accompanying me took the nerves down a bit. I called him back.

"Uh, on second thought. I'll go but...Sarah is coming

also. Is that okay?"

"Sure. I'll have Tim tag along. So what does it take, forty minutes for you to meet in Coral Cove?"

"Yes, about."

"Okay. See you then."

* * *

Thursday was here. Anticipation tickled my feet all day, nervously counting down the hours until I was to meet Jack. What was I doing tonight? Going to dinner—with a customer. *No. I was breaking all my own rules! Relax.* I would go to dinner and have a few glasses of wine. Nerve diffusers.

I pick up Sarah and we hit 95 north. I fuss with my hair and makeup the entire trip.

"Look at you. You're a basket case. You look fine." Sarah says, rolling her eyes.

" I don't know what's up with me." I brush the hair out of my face.

"You might like him...a little."

"Nah, fat chance. I like talking to him though. Let's see how this goes."

* * *

"Hey girls." Jack calls, waving us into the booth.

Sarah takes her side next to Tim, and I next to Jack. Totally looked double date with younger girls. Well what did it matter? We' d never see this server again. I study Jack, looking much different from that night in the club. Charcoal slacks and a royal blue dress shirt that highlighted the roundness of his belly. A Breitling watch peeks out from under the cuff. His dark brown hair neatly groomed, parted to one side.

"What would you girls like to drink?" Jack asks as we close in on an appetizer of spinach and artichoke dip. Taking a glass of Pinot Noir, I hide behind the glass. Sitting there beside him, I stopped hearing his words and get lost in his mouth. It was beautiful, with tight Romanesque lips that curled ever so slightly at the corners. He was the epitome of some high-powered bigwig. The starched shirt, the crease in his slack, even the polished shoes; everything about him screamed methodical.

Tim was on the road to singledom, going through divorce proceedings upon discovering his wife's affair. I tried to show compassion to this dire news but left that job to Sarah. I was more interested on what was going on with this side of the table.

"So you guys don't actually feel anything when you're dancing do you?" Jack asks.

"No, not really. It's a job you know? Well then again, there are some girls that do get off on dancing for a guy, or even do more for a guy. That's when a fight ensues." I say.

"You guys have fights in there?" Jack's eyebrows shoot up.

"On occasion. It's usually when a girl is acting like a whore. Doing stuff she shouldn't be doing."

Sarah nods in agreement.

"Like what?" I felt like I was on an interview all of a sudden. Jack had this childlike curiosity about the camaraderie among us girls. Why I don't know.

"Sexual favors for money. It's not supposed to be like that. It's supposed to be nothing more than an erotic, sensual dance. But some girls do more. Those are usually the pill heads. They're willing to do anything to fix a habit. That all the more feeds into the negative stereotype with dancers."

I take a scoop of spinach artichoke dip.

"So you both live in Marble?" Jack asks. Tim was lost in caressing Sarah's shoulders.

"Yes, I live right by the inter coastal waterway in a gated community. It's only about fifteen minutes away from the beach. I'm there often."

"And what about you?" Jack asks Sarah.

"I'm more inland than she is, but only about ten minutes from her place."

Why was he so interested on my whereabouts?

"Cool. Must be nice to have the ocean breeze in close reach. We don't have that where we live."

"Oh? Well where in Marsh Harbor do you guys live?" I asked.

"The southwest side."

Flop. Well that really told me a lot. Marsh Harbor was the largest city in north Florida. So he was vague with regard to his own life but oddly curious about mine. It was going on eight, and the blue cloak of night was closing in.

* * *

I come outside to see Jack pacing back and forth in the parking lot, two white envelopes clutched in his hand.

"Come over here for a second."

"Yeah?"

"$400 for you, and $200 for Sarah. Was fun tonight." Pushing the envelopes tightly into my hand, I accept them, but not without some trepidation.

"Are you serious?" I look up to him, wide eyed.

"Just wanted you to be compensated for your time. There's some gas money in there as well."

"You know you don't have to do this."

"I know I don't."

I stand there abashedly, finishing his statement in my head. He knows he doesn't have to, but he *can*. Waiting for Sarah and Tim to come out, Jack finagles with his phone. His fingers widened the geographical area and a map appeared. I realized he was studying Marble Beach.

"What are you doing?" I asked playfully, craning my neck.

"Just browsing the inter coastal area."

"This must be your apartment complex right here right?" He said, pointing to the map.

A satellite image of a gated complex with tan buildings appeared, right on the river. Surprised but shocked, I muttered, "Yes. That would be it."

"Huh. Well that's not far from the club at all. You just basically go up here, go over the bridge and you're on A1A."

"Yep."

I knew what he was doing. He didn't care about how far it was from the club. That was just a cover. He just wanted to see where I lived. *Stalker*. But at the same time, I found it flattering. Why did he want to know so badly where I lived? Let alone even cared?

"Hey guys," Tim and Sarah come out.

"Well, it's getting late. Better start heading home. It was fun." Jack said.

Unsure whether to hug him or not, I trip over my own feet, giving him an awkward pat on the back embrace.

"You sure there wasn't something in that wine?" Tim chimed in.

Brushing the hair from my face, my eyes met Jack's.

"Thank you very much for tonight."

"It was very much my pleasure." Those blue eyes sink into me, and those mere five minutes or so saying our goodbyes seem strangely longer.

"Well this beats working!" Sarah proclaims, fanning through the bills as we head home. Counting mine, there wasn't a dollar less, not a dollar more.

"Well he wanted to compensate us for our time. He did just that, and then some."

5

May 2011

The placid tickle of summer days provides an invitation to wake boarding, picnics and outdoor activities. Beaches fill. Ice cream stands gain more customers. The gardenia bushes that border my apartment perfume the air as I walk out to fetch my mail. My mailbox usually consisted of a few revolving pieces of paper: cable bill, electric bill, the occasional magazine subscription. But a smooth, white business envelope with my name scribbled in blue ink caught my attention.

I plop down on my sofa and study it. A mixture of caps and lowercase. Hard-pressed ink. I open it and out falls $200. *What the—oh my god, Jack.* So this was why he'd been so adamant about my location the other day. Why was he sending me money—and through the postal service at that? Was he crazy? Someone could have easily torn this open and had a field day. I text him immediately.

*Are you crazy sending money in the mail? And what's this for?

Within minutes a response.

*I figured I'd send $100 a day for walk around cash, especially if you don't feel like going to work.

Wait. What? Why? My head floods with questions. Any other girl in my position would lap this up, but from the day I moved out at the ripe age of twenty, years of independence had stubbornly obstructed my view. Everything I'd accumulated was due to my tenacious work ethic. I couldn't accept this. Why was he doing this?

"Listen, it's just some cash for groceries and what not." Jack says over the phone on his way home from work.

"Two hundred dollars? What do you think I'm feeding, an army?"

"Will you just relax? Do me a favor. Don't ask why. Just take it."

Flabbergasted, I ignored his request.

"But—"

"So how do you feel about a coffee later this week? I think Thursday I free up around five."

The man was a pro at changing the subject.

"Thursday? Sure. Okay."

"Okay, well," another phone rang in the background. "This is work. I've gotta run. Have a good night."

It was at that moment I realized that Jack operated on two phones. For the past few months I had blindly assumed called me from just one. But he had two—one for me, the other for the home front. *Holy shit this guy was something else.* But where did he hide it? At work? At home?

I drape myself on my sofa. Candles dance along the wall as Frank Sinatra's "Wives and Lovers" played on Pandora. Staring up at the ceiling, I mouthed the words while Jack invaded my mind.

Hey, little girl, comb your hair, fix your make-up, soon he will open the door,

Don't think because there's a ring on your finger, you needn't try any more.

For wives should always be lovers too,

Run to his arms the moment that he comes home to you.

I'm warning you,

Day after day, there are girls at the office and the men will always be men,

Don't stand him up, with your hair still in curlers, you may not see him again.

* * *

"Fuck!" It's Thursday and I'm sitting among a trail of mascara-blotted Q-tips before my mirror.

"Okay, let's try this again." I blurt out loud. I was particularly struggling today. My hair spewed a weird cowlick and it seemed one eye had more shadow on than the other. Nerves? Probably. I tame my hair the best I can and sprint out the door.

Jack sits languidly at a small table, lost in an outstretched *New York Times*. His 6'5" frame was still towering even while cradled in the chair. I order a white mocha and drag my gelatin limbs to his table.

"Hey you."

Kept

"Hi. Beautiful out today."

"Yeah, too bad I didn't get to enjoy most of it."

I began to notice a solemn connotation anytime work was brought into the conversation. And although I was still unclear as to what he did for a living, I presumed there was a corporate utopia, one of which possibly consisted of endless emails and deadlines and conference calls. One where, people didn't necessarily welcome him with open arms, but rather dispersed like cattle when he entered a room. I presumed he was high up on the corporate totem pole, perhaps had people who reported to him. He pulls out a small piece of scrap paper from his pocket.

"Do me a favor. Write down all of your monthly expenses."

I rest my temple on my index finger. "What?"

"You heard me," He pressed. "Go ahead. Everything. Your rent, your car, car insurance, phone, credit cards. I want to know what kind of numbers we're working with."

We're? He made it sound like we were in business together. Once again my head became cloudy. Why did he care? Didn't he have his own family to worry about? I stared at the blank piece of paper, and then began writing.

41

Rent- $550

Car- $449

Electric- $50

Health insurance- $134

Car insurance- $62

Credit cards- $4,000 (combined total of two balances)

I slip him the piece of paper.

"Alright. Not bad. Do you have a bank account?"

I chuckled at his inquiry. "Of course I do. It is 2011 after all."

His eyebrows shot up at my sass. "Okay. What do you have, just a checking and a savings?"

"Yes. As for savings, not much in there."

"Okay. Write down the balances."

He slid the paper back to me. I didn't quite understand why he wanted these, but I jot them down anyway.

"Okay. Not bad. You've got at least $500 in checking, savings could use a little help. But you probably just spent a lot of that in Zurich huh?"

"Precisely. But worth every penny."

"Oh yeah, I don't doubt it. You don't hear about too
many girls in your business saving their money for some
European excursion."

I nod agreeably.

"I have more fruitful conquests to embark on than some
Xanax."

His eyes darted down to his Breitling, then outside, and
then back to me.

"Gotta run. Here's some gas money. Enjoyed it; wish it
could've been longer."

"Okay. Bye." Wow. Well that was an abrupt exit. I count
the money. $200. *Oh my god*. Finishing the last few sips
of my mocha, I tried to understand why those last twenty
minutes or so left me feeling lifted and minutely happy,
even if our time together was constrained. Just to see
him was enough to brighten the remainder of my day.
Walking out to my car, my phone rings.

"Hey. So I want you to take that $200 I gave you, leave
out $100 for walk around and deposit the rest in the
bank. I want to build up your savings."

Ah, savings. Such a nice ring to it, but oh-so-hard to build if you had one too many slow nights. Granted I had mustered to save enough for my trip to Zurich, but the most I'd ever managed to put away was a measly $4,000.

"Okay."

"Oh and one more thing. Don't you have any student loans from that previous school you attended for phlebotomy?"

Damn. He didn't miss a beat.

"Oh. Yes, actually, but they're not in repayment yet."

"Do you know how much you owe?"

"Probably around $9,000."

"Okay. Look into that and give me the balance."

"Will do."

His other phone rang in the background.

"Shit. This is work, gotta go. Have a good night and be safe."

I hang up and my eyes get lost in the road on the way back to Marble Beach. I felt hazy, lost in a daze of a million whys as I struggled to make sense of his inherent need to assist me..

* * *

Friday was filled with errands, mostly of the financial kind. I checked my student loan balance and made a stop to the bank. I stocked up on some groceries, paying for them with Jack's money. Wow, not paying for my *own* groceries? I smacked down a growing pang of peculiarity. Well he doesn't care, so why should I?

* * *

5:00 in the evening. I pace in my living room anticipating his call. Jack's fluctuating hours had me wondering how smoothly that went over at home. It became clear to me how these sporadic hours made for an easily deceptive front. He probably had a treasury of excuses: a client dinner, a conference call that ran over, whatever. This intermittent schedule seemingly helped him out to slip between two worlds—fantasy and reality.

"I don't want you to go into work tonight." Jack chants through the phone. It was a Friday and I usually could be found in the bathroom curling my hair at this hour, doing the transformation for the night ahead. Instead, I'm having a tit-for-tat with him about going in or not. The weekends were our busiest nights and I always took advantage of them, rarely ever going out for fun. I always worked.

"It's a Friday. I always work Fridays."

Who was he to tell me or more or less—*order* me—to go into work or not?

"Just go to some bar with Sarah tonight, flirt with some boys."

My eyes narrowed. "What?"

There was an air of self-deprecation in his words. I knew better over the past few months that it couldn't be any further from what he truly wanted.

"I know you enjoy the performing part of the job—the pole dancing— but to be honest, I can't stand the thought of you being in that atmosphere."

Put off by his fervor I find myself stuck, unsure of what the next move was. And then he makes the decision for me.

"I want some texts tonight of whatever you do. Go have some fun."

And then he was gone. I wouldn't talk to him until the morning.

"What the fuck?" I sigh out loud. I didn't get it. *Why? How? Is this the new normal?* What is *this*? I had a guy with apparently more money than he knew what to do with, willingly sending me little white envelopes in the mail and ordering me not to work. Yeah, this kind of shit happens to everyday people.

I glance at my nightstand with the butterfly clipped $200 there. Well, I guess I wasn't going in tonight. I gather myself and head out for some comfort in a bottle—to the liquor store. I wasn't much of a drinker but tonight I wanted some nerve diffusers. My brain felt exhausted. I wanted to numb this merry-go-round of fleeting questions.

* * *

I return with a bottle of Pinot and light some candles. I swish it around in my mouth, and let it roll off the tongue as it helps my reverberating thoughts to fade. What did he want from me? Obviously it wasn't sex. If that were so he would've made a move already, only to be shot down with flying colors. There was a lot about him that I admired though too. The fact that sexual innuendo was absent from our conversations was refreshing to me. He made me feel like a real woman, not one that he'd met in the club. Not one defined by her job.

6

Monday. I hadn't done much this past weekend except for getting acquainted with the woodsy notes of Pinot, a walk along the beach on Sunday and what I was presently doing: standing at my mailbox glowering at yet another envelope in that same hard-pressed ink with a mix of caps and lowercase. Out falls $400.

I can't believe him. I mean it's not like I'm *asking* for this. Jack's searing blue eyes burn into my mind and I head to the bank, making a deposit into my savings.

My days of working five nights a week began to dwindle. Any other girl in my position would have just sworn off work altogether but I couldn't do that. I still went, just not as often as I had once did.

I'd never relied on anyone for money. It felt foreign and institutionalized. Why wasn't I feeling like the money-grubbing herd of girls I worked with? Many of them would have happily accepted this, resorting to a life of handsomely paid couch potatoes. And here I was, struggling with the concept.

He actually wanted me to go out on a Friday and Saturday and simply, have fun—and I would be compensated for it. On those weekend nights where I began to venture out, I tried to stifle his presence, but he was always there, lurking in the corners of my mind. He made himself impossible to forget. I found myself completely flummoxed.

Kept

7

I meet Jack at *Keke's*, a quaint dinner spot. Our time together, although I never expected much given the state of things, was increasing. There were weekly dinners and coffee dates. Hundreds—if not thousands—of dollars for my time since February. He was undoubtedly a busy man with his hours being sporadic, but this all the more catered to his chicanery.

"So how was your day?" Jack smiles as he peels back the pages of *Money* magazine.

"Good. Just did a few errands, rather boring actually."

"Cool, cool," He fans through the emails on his phone and nods.

My usually effortless conversational talents flat-lined as I frantically search for something to add to the silent air. With each meeting, I increasingly found myself intrigued of his presence and its uncanny ability to rob me of my words. We exit the restaurant and I follow behind Jack, always weary of our public distance.

"Hold out your hand."

Shoving a wad of hundreds secured with a butterfly clip, I stare at the money, stupefied.

"That's for rent and car. Go do those errands tomorrow. Call you in a few."

Oh my god. There's $1,200 here. This is why he'd been probing. This was the reason for that list of expenses.

* * *

I follow a long line of traffic home. It was raining and Floridians seem to lose their depth perception whenever a single drop hit the ground. The phone rings.

"Alright so. This is what I want you to do: there's $450 for your car payment and $550 for your rent. Any extra is walk around cash or just deposit it in the bank. Go take care of those chores tomorrow, got it?"

"Yeah… got it."

I listen intently to Jack's businesslike tenor in what he referred to as 'chores'. *This is my life. What the fuck.*

* * *

The aroma of coffee fills my living room and I relish a moment of silence, staring at the $1,200 sitting on the counter. *Goddamn that was a lot of money.*

And then a text:

*Chores done?

*Send balances.

8

"What does your calendar look like for June 6th, 7th and 8th?"

My car payment and rent had both been taken care of, and increasingly absent from my mind was the frantic end of the month jitters. I mindlessly push a pile of soggy asparagus around on my plate, sitting at lunch with Jack. Looking up to those icy blue depths, so many questions for them. But more so what was encouraged was acceptance, not analysis.

"Um nothing I suppose. Why? What's on those dates?"

"I've got to go to Dallas for business." "Okay and this concerns me how?" I loved playing coy. "Was going to see if you'd like to tag along."

"What?" My fork hits my plate.

"Well I thought since you like to travel, and you've never seen Dallas, thought I'd ask."

"What about work? I've got to work."

"You'd be compensated for the days you're away from the club. $200 a day sound fair?"

Hm. I liked where his head was at.

"How would I be getting around?"

"I'd get you a rental car."

I tried to piece together this business deal for lack of a better term.

"I don't know."

"What don't you know about? Three days in a new city, expenses paid."

"I just don't know. Because, I—I can't."

Words escaped me like some punch-drunk lexicon salad.

I pushed around the asparagus, looking down at my plate like some scolded child. I didn't want to look up at the face of disdain before me.

"Right, because I have time to waste. Let me tell you something. I'm old, I don't have time to waste."

At thirty-nine, Jack had me by thirteen years.

"Thirty-nine isn't old. That's all in your head. Maybe it's your job that's aging you." I said, smirking.

"Tell you what. Why don't you go home tonight and think about it. We're just shy of two weeks out, so I don't want to waste much more time in booking. Look at the early morning flights. 7:30 is when I'm flying out. I will text you later."

Sliding out of the booth, he slips me $200 and we part ways.

* * *

Cradled in my bed, I patiently wait for my sluggish HP to pull up a window. The thing was six years old and had seen better days. A thunderstorm raged on outside as raindrops angrily pelted my window.

*Find any flights out for 7:30?

I look at the time. 10:30. How was he texting me right

now? Why aren't you doing the family thing?

*Yes, I saw the 7:30. #1247?

*Yes. Grab it.

My index finger hovers over the purchase icon. How do I know he's not playing with me building up some jet-set diorama in my mind? I text him back.

*How do I know you're serious?

Five long minutes.

*Like I said before, I've got no time to waste. If it helps, my seat is 20B. You can look it up and see if it's taken. Your call.

While he wasn't exactly pressuring me per se, his words were threaded with a coaxing factor. My mind drifts to accommodations. What would I do about that? Where would I be staying? He surely didn't think I'd be staying with him—in his room, in his bed—did he?

*Where would I be staying?

*The Fielmont.

Holy crap, he *was* serious.

I Google the address. Yep, it existed. I marveled at

photos of the place, Fielmont properties were always pretty nice anyway. I felt my doubts begin to dissipate.

*I can pay for my own room.

*Are you serious? You're not paying for anything. You'll have your own room.

I could almost hear his scoffing through text.

*Just grab the #1247 and room. Gotta run.

My eyes blink on autopilot at the screen. Well if I did go, I'd get my own room so that was comforting. And if he turned out to be some sadomasochistic maniac or worse yet, a murderer, I could always outrun him. *What the fuck am I doing?*

* * *

Any other Sunday would have likely been spent at the beach for my evening jog. Instead I headed north to Marsh Harbor to crash in an airport hotel given the painfully early wake up call tomorrow: 5:00 A.M. A time that usually found me just creeping underneath the sheets following a night at work.

I arrive at the hotel ravenous, pouring over the in-room dining menu. I hadn't heard from Jack yet today. The very small chance of him standing me up lurks in the back of my mind but I shoot it down, shaking my head at my overactive imagination.

I return back to my room following a very basic meal at a Cracker Barrel beside the hotel. I sit surrounded in the cold silence of this hotel room, transfixed by the blue fluorescence of the television as I nurse a beer. I look at the time: 11:30. Within a mere eight hours, I would be boarding a plane with Jack, a man whom I had become peculiarly drawn to, despite the fact that he was elusive as fuck.

My concentration efforts flat line and this besetting mental countdown in my head ticks by at the hours and minutes left. How did I know he wasn't some fruit loop hiding behind a mask of charisma? How did I know he'd even be aboard that plane tomorrow morning? I unlock the door and with car keys in hand, stare at my car. *I want to leave. I should go. This is not right. Why am I here? What am I doing? I don't have to go anywhere.* But the charge—the charge for the room, the hotel—it's on my card. Shit.

Kept

9

*Awake?

It was Jack. A strange rush of relief and elation takes over my body. I look at the time. Oh my god. 4:45 A.M.

Suddenly the worrying, the analyzing—all of it—came to a halt.

*Yes

*See you soon.

And there, I had my answer. He was, and had been serious, after all.

* * *

I'm sitting at C9 in front of the floor to ceiling glass windows as I watch the night taper off, the cool blue of early morning filtering in. I see Jack moving cautiously down the corridor, a few minutes behind me. His head cocks left to right, nonchalantly surveying the atmosphere. Folding the *Wall Street Journal* under his arm, he takes a seat across from me.

I sit there silent, guarded by my ear buds, saving me from any conversation. My lips curl up. I smile at many things, not just the unforeseen adventure that lay ahead, but also the man who stood before me, a man who had become many things to me. In almost five months time, Jack had morphed from patron, to financial advisor, to friend, to someone whose company I had come to enjoy.

"American Airlines flight #1247 now boarding group A passengers."

10

A cordial bellhop of about fifty greets me as I move through the carousel door, his salt and pepper hair ruffling in the arid Texas breeze.

"Morning ma'am, welcome to the Fielmont. Would you like any help with that?"

His deep crows feet suggest a lifetime of smiley greetings he had done here.

"I am okay but thank you." I say as I nervously move past him.

I bring myself to the concierge; Jack stands a few rows down. A cherry redheaded associate named Molly greets me.

"So what brings you to Dallas, Miss Arbour?"

How intrusive. Or maybe it wasn't. Perhaps it was my own paranoia creeping up over an otherwise innocuous question.

"Oh just business." I reply.

"Oh ok. Alright, here's your room key. You will be on the fifth floor. Breakfast is served in the dining room from 6:30 until 11:00. Will you need a city guide?"

"I think I'm good. Thank you."

I walk to the elevators, passing by Jack like I don't know him. I study my reflection in the bronze doors as it gurgles up five floors. My dark auburn hair swept up in a bun, I stare at myself: knee-high boots, tights and a billowy top. I clearly wasn't here for business.

Following a buttercream striped winding hallway, I enter my room and perch myself along an alcove that overlooks a glittering pond below. And then the phone.

*You all settled in? What room are you in?

*The fifth.

Right on. *Do you have to get to the office?

*Yes but I have time for lunch.

I was running on fumes. My early morning Starbucks

concoction had long since worn off.

*Okay. Meet me in the lobby in fifteen.

Jack rarely fashioned his sentences as questions. They were more like suggestions with a commanding undertone.

* * *

"So you ever take a plane to lunch before?" Jack asks. We're sitting in a spot called the Fiery Chef that totes everything I don't eat: burgers, fries, you know…man food.

"Definitely not."

"Told you you'd be on that plane. You were probably all nervous stewing in your room weren't you?"

My mouth gapes open.

"Maybe."

"Well this is Jack's world. It's a bit different from the

rest of the world."

We finish lunch and while I could have explored Dallas that day, I went directly to my room, huddling there in a ball of anxiety for the next five hours until Jack left the office.

A bottle of opened wine with a Fielmont sleeve sits on the alcove, I look out to the Dallas skyline as I sip. There were so many thoughts that I just wanted to put on mute: *why was I here? What am I doing? This is so wrong. But I'm not doing anything. I haven't done anything. I am in my room, alone. Nothing has happened. Nothing will happen. I am in control of anything happening. If he tries anything, that's it, gone. Back home. Right? Right.*

11

Brimstone was ranked high in the hierarchy of Dallas' notorious steak houses. Walls drenched in masculine cherry wood and burgundy upholstered booths, the whispers and expressions of each conversation were illuminated a pale yellow by the flicker of candlelight perched along every table.

"So what did you see today? Anything good?" Jack asks.

"No, I was kind of tired."

"Tired? I gave you car so you could go explore."

"I know, I know. Don't worry Dallas isn't going anywhere."

"I had about six meetings today, one after the other, with a bunch of smelly Indian customer service reps."

"Oh that sounds treacherous."

"It was. But now here I am with a beautiful woman. So have you ever taken a plane to dinner?"

"Do you use the same question twice?" I tease.

"Oh, someone is observant."

"Among other things."

A sommelier refills our glasses with their best Pinot Noir.

"Uh, definitely never taken a plane to dinner. So that makes two meals now that I've flown in for." I roll my eyes coyly, sips becoming more like awkward gulps and eyes playing an erratic dance pattern from table to wall and back again, all to avoid Jack's looming stare. I hadn't drunk this much in one day in who knows when.

Our server arrives with our meal of filet, asparagus and mushrooms à la carte. We order another bottle. I feel my inhibitions begin to melt away and the throbbing cloud of questions begin to fall out of my mouth, a nagging need to answer the presumptions I've harbored for months manifests itself right on the white cloth table.

"You know what's the mystery of life? Keeping shit fresh, like marriage. Marriage intimidates the hell out of me. I don't know if I'll ever do it."

My eyes dart to couple punch drunk on PDA, arms entangled and sharing wine-infused smooches.

"Couldn't agree more." Jack nods, and we share a toast. His blue eyes cast a cool grey that hooked me as I hid behind my glass.

"And what about you?"

"What about me?" Jack loved to deflect.

"Well, there's got to be *some* degree of void in your life. Why else would you fly a girl you hardly know on a business trip to Dallas?"

The silence between us grows. Pushing his asparagus around on his plate, his eyes scan the table as he gathers an answer.

"Well, she just kind of does her thing and I do mine." "You don't see each other much?"

"No not really, unless it's the kids' sports games or something."

"Wow."

Jack shrugs his shoulders. "Yeah. It is what it is."

We finish dinner and I polish off what I think was my fifth glass of wine. I'd admittedly lost count at this point, taken by this aperture into his feverishly hidden life.

Camille Lindstrom

12

I glance at my key card. My room was on the fifth floor but here I was, in his. But the feeling wasn't standoffish. Instead it felt natural. That could be the wine. Perhaps most of it could be because of the wine. Okay a lot of it was because of the wine. *I'm not having sex with him. I'm not having sex with him. I'm not having sex with him.*

The room aglow with the blue flicker of the television, the city lights of Dallas glitter outside below. My eyelids play a rhythmic dance of open and close and I begin to drift off in the nook of Jack's arm. Cold and methodical, his eyes lie fixed on me, without the slightest hint of fatigue. Together in this moment, there's a mutual silence, curiosity and desire hangs in the air as our breath intermingles.

My eyes shoot open with a sudden trace of Jack's finger gliding down my midriff, tracing a path down to my hipbones, up the middle of my chest and to my shoulder. Bodies grazing each other, he pulls me closer. *Oh no, is he going to kiss me? No, no, no.* My legs flail. I try to roll back from him but he pulls me close. My body awash in titillation, his lips meet mine.

* * *

I sit in the dining room of the Fielmont. Cold eggs and a croissant sit before me, untouched. *What the hell happened last night?*

And then the phone.

*Good morning. Last night was great.

*We kissed was all. Right?

*We did, you were shaking like a leaf.

Oh my god. I can't believe what I'm reading. This is everything I did not want to do.

*Left you some money for walk around. Deposit it to the bank and don't be late to the airport. Flight leaves around 6:00 pm.

I didn't do much for those last few hours in Dallas. My mind was cluttered with what this was—or what this was becoming.

* * *

"Ladies and gentlemen, the pilot has begun his initial descent into the Marsh Harbor area. Please stow away all tray tables and electronics."

For the last two hours I'd studied the mannerisms of Jack as he sat a few rows ahead of me. Although he had opened up just a little over dinner at Brimstone, my mind still fought for answers, and a thousand whys circled my brain.

13

Sept. 2011

The envelopes continued, about one per week.
Sometimes two. Bank trips became so frequent that I had
struck up a kind of rapport with the tellers where I was
on a first name basis. My stubborn nature upon reception
lessened. I still worked, but my typical four to five days
a week had dwindled down to two. I would be in Dallas
again on Tuesday, for yet another "work trip."

Usually 7:00 A.M would have found me
motionless and dead to the world in my bed, but the
increasingly familiar pattern of these early morning
flights had my once nocturnal feeding hours falling to
the wayside. By now we had had that "two assuming
strangers" guise down pat.

Shuffling down the terminal, I spot Jack sitting cool and collected, flipping through the *Wall Street Journal.*

"Boarding group B, please." Sounded the PA.

Jack saunters by me, but not too close.

"Hey. Real quick, I know about four people on this flight; so…James Bond stance, alright?"

I nod. Boarding the plane, I pass Jack's row, cold and unassuming, adopting the same degree of distance as our last trip. I take my seat.

*I work with the man behind you.

Oh my god. Eyes rolling, I sink into my seat.

* * *

We sit in the swanky throes of Saffron, one of Dallas' luxe global cuisine spots. The place is undoubtedly beautiful, flanked in alabaster walls and equally adorned white tabletops. I sit in a tailored green sheath, fidgeting with my clutch, giving me something to do with my clammy hands.

Jack sits with his head tilted over his phone, punching the keys.

"God, these guys just don't get it. It's like you've got to tell them five different ways to do the same thing. I feel like I've got idiots working for me sometimes."

I grab the bottle of Shiraz sitting on our table and give a generous pour.

"Wine?"

"No. Something stronger. Hey buddy," he whistles to the waiter.

"Give me a dirty martini, up. Thanks."

Shoving the phone in his pocket, Jack cracks a smile as his drink arrives. "So, don't we look beautiful tonight?"

"I do what I can." I say, blushing, and we toast glasses.

Just another trip to Dallas…

14

We stumble back into the room and fall into the sheets. Reclining into each other's arms, one kiss turns into twenty. I am hungry for him, our mouths engulfing each other. The wine streams through my veins and I feel weightless. He throws me down on the bed. Jack's shaky fingers peruse the bend of my thigh and my underwear is peeled down my ankles. *What was happening? Everything that I didn't want to. But I didn't stop it.*

My hands cup his face, our bodies hungrily examining each other. I wanted to unmask the heavily guarded man before me. The fascination for him was so strong in this moment that any sense of time had become seemingly absent. The only thing constantly moving was a fondness; a fondness enriched with time. Holding a silent stare at each other, his heavy frame overtook me. My legs inched wider and wider apart, and months of repressed desire finally culminated as I let out one piercing moan.

My head cradled in the cold concave of the pillow, my body lie outstretched as I let him take me, the surrounding dark of the room swallowing our gasps. With each thrust, my legs interlock as I hold his face by the temples, cheeks grazing mine as my eyes tore into his, those icy blue depths sharing the same look of trepidation as mine. And then with one deep push, he came. Descending from my euphoria, a mental fog of purples, greens and darkness splinter from my psyche as the room comes back into focus. Cupping my cheek, he kisses my forehead.

"How do you feel?"

"I'm okay."

Perhaps it's safe to say we both had our own respective qualms. But at that moment, we essentially became the very things that we did not want.

Looking up at him, I couldn't wipe the disdain from my eyes. "You're not supposed to be –this...this is not supposed to be."

* * *

I lie on my living room floor staring up at the ceiling. My suitcase lies on the living room floor; souvenirs and dirty clothes wait to be organized. The Radio Dept. plays in the background and I sit motionless on the floor. I was so transfixed by what had happened on this second trip to Dallas. Everything that I had wanted *not* to. I had only been home for a few hours, Jack and I parting ways discreetly in the parking deck of the Marsh Harbor airport hours before. I looked to the counter where $700 stood. What was I? A girlfriend? A travel companion? Some would easily say whore by now. Shit. It's not like I ever *asked* him to give me money, he just did. I guess that was his way of taking care of what I would've missed had I gone to work.

A pang of guilt struck my gut. I thought of the wife. I could be her. I could be married to a guy who pulls this kind of double life charade but be blissfully unaware in my sprawling homestead while I revel in country club dates with other neighborhood housewives. What was worse?

15

January 2012

"We've got an office right on Park Ave. I usually have to report here at least once a year. Some of my guys are at this office."

I remember that midnight conversation over the summer of last year. Jack had called me while he was on a business trip in New York City. We talked about my wanderlust, and how it had never taken me to the concrete jungle—at least not yet. At that time, I was still in the dark as to what exactly he did for a living, and now here I was, on another plane to another city.

While we usually flew American to Dallas, Delta

was a change of pace. We didn't meet at our old standby C9, our friendly passport to Dallas once every month or two. This plane up to LaGuardia was significantly smaller, with Jack ducking his head as he shuffled down the cramped aisle to his seat. I smirked as he passed me by.

"Your first time to the city?" My seatmate asks, a black woman of about sixty.

"Yes, I'm excited. I'll be here for three days. I travel a lot, but I've never been to New York."

"So what brings you there?"

"Oh, friends. Lucky bastards, living in the city and all."

This was a recurring question I'd learned to tackle with grace all these months of living out of suitcases and hotel jumping with Jack.

"Very nice child, well you enjoy yourself in the city."

And before she could inquire about further details, in went the ear buds as I closed my eyes for a while on the two and a half hour leg up.

* * *

A parade of yellow cabs greet us outside the Delta terminal at LaGuardia, lined up in a competitive brigade, all fighting for customers.

Jack slips me a small piece of paper and a few hundred dollars in my hand. We disperse.

"Here's the hotel address. Don't forget to tip the driver well. See you soon."

Throwing my bags into the backseat, my very first cab ride in New York is a stinky one. This cab smells of wilted cabbage and body odor. Jack hops into a black car ahead.

"Hi, the Intercontinental please."

My cab driver was a twenty something Bangladeshi kid, a bit shy but welcoming.

"Ah, that's a nice hotel. What brings you to the city?"

"Uh, business."

"What do you do?"

I had become quick on my feet and full of shit when strangers asked questions.

"Charters enterprises. We have a site here in Manhattan. Park Avenue to be exact."

"Nice. Well there's a TV back there for your enjoyment. With traffic, it will probably be about twenty minutes."

I didn't look at the TV. My head was too busy hanging out the window in the grey dismal rain, the spellbinding enormity of New York catching me with my mouth wide open as we crossed the Williamsburg Bridge.

* * *

I help myself to the hotel bar, arriving first. Sipping a glass of cabernet, I study the hotel. The décor of the Intercontinental echoed back to its 1920's heyday. Cherry wood pillars towered over Victorian furniture in subdued reds, greens and blues, accompanied by dimly lit lamps under which hotel guests sat with their laptops. There was a palpable coldness that hung in the air among the hotel patrons, everyone busy, immersed in their own world, wrapped in business meetings and hurriedly replying to emails. But then again we were in the city that never sleeps.

"Hey there. How was your first cab ride? Did you use the oh-shit handles?"

I turned around to see Jack.

"The what?"

"The handles in the back. They're to hold on. These cabbies make it seem like its NASCAR in the city sometimes."

"I see. I will remember that." I chuckled.

The Intercontinental was a 685-room hotel in the heart of Manhattan, between 48th and 49th, bordered by Park Avenue and Lexington. Like most New York real estate, the only option was to build was up, not out. And so, when taking this popular New York stipulation into account, the scant measurements of our room suddenly made sense. The room was very simple: a king bed, a desk, TV, and a small bathroom, which Jack fit into, albeit barely. But it didn't matter, as neither of us would be spending much time in there anyway. Jack would be over on Park Avenue in and out of meetings, and I would be jumping cab to cab, exploring the city on my own.

"Here's $700. Want you to find a bank, deposit $300 to cover the airfare; the rest should cover you for cabs, food, and souvenirs. Should free up around 3:00, I'll be in touch. Have fun, be safe."

Hugging my waist, Jack plants a few kisses on me before he joins the maze of people that scurry below.

Looking out from our ninth story window, I get lost in
the velocity of the city, a cacophony of yells and honks
and the clouds of steam that billow from the sewer
drains.

* * *

Stashing the money deep down in my knee-high boot, I
adjust my scarf and tuck my disheveled hair under a
beret. It was cold out. I throw my camera into my purse
and welcome the gritty invitation that is New York.

Walking outside into the cold wet of January, I'd
prepared myself to study the art of hailing down a cab;
only I didn't have to. A line of bellhops stand outside the
entrance to the hotel, decked out in black and grey trench
coats bellowing a language of nuanced whistles. A
bellhop with a peppery mustache and rumpled eyes
approaches me. He'd been at this a long time, it was
written all over his face.

"Where you off to?"

I look frantically at the list I'd made of places to hit up.

"Um, the MOMA."

Together with two fingers pressed hard on his tongue, he
belts out a most discernible call, undulating with a sharp

hook at the end. The thing seemed to bounce off the neighboring buildings. I slip the guy $5 and hop into a cab. This one luckily didn't stink. A few torrential city blocks later, I arrive at the Metropolitan Museum of Modern Art only to be met with disappointment. A monstrous line wraps around the perimeter of the cold, gray building. With six hours to spare, I decided I'd hit that on another day, and took a stab at hailing down a cab. Across the street, a man waves one arm in the air, yelling "Taxi!"

I follow suit, but they all pass me by. *What the fuck?* And then I realize: the rooftop lights were off, signaling 'Out of Service'. *Tourist.*

After awhile, I finally flag one down.

"Hi, where you headed?" The driver asks.

"Times Square please."

I was in New York. I had to pay at least one visit to the tourist mecca of the Big Apple. The cab weasels in and out of traffic, the abrupt stops and turns making the seatbelt into a strangulation device. This time I hold on to the oh-shit handles. Having no concept of what an appropriate tip was for a cabbie, I slip him $10 as he speeds away, honking his horn as he's swallowed up in the rat race of cabs. I stand in the middle of Times Square. Thousands of people stop to pose for photos, buy souvenirs and share in this equally enigmatic moment. The energy here unlike anything I'd ever seen before. Sparkling neon signs that blinked and flashed set the streets aglow. Pedestrians here were a colorful contrast from the stoic businessman of Manhattan, adopting a more thespian look. After all, this was where many Broadway shows were done.

I glance at my watch. It was going on 6:00. Jack wouldn't be out of his last meeting until 7:00. I make my way back to the Intercontinental on foot, block by block in the slushy ambiance of the city. The cabs moved too fast and I wanted to see everything, like the homeless guy before me with a sign proclaiming, "Liquor and cocaine!" I threw him a few bucks. At least he was honest.

16

"Hey you, you sleeping?"

The door shuts behind Jack, waking me up from a nap.

"Oh, hey."

"How long have you been out?"

"Oh man, I don't even know. Maybe forty-five minutes?"

Loosening his collar and unbuttoning his cuffs, he collapses in an oversized Victorian armchair that stood in front of the only window in the room. His arms reach out for me like a child, and I plop myself in his lap, rubbing his temples.

"I love your touch," he says, smiling. "You hungry?"

* * *

Luna Piena was a narrow sliver of authentic Italian goodness off E. 53rd. With the two of us sitting at a dimly lit table as our waiter approached, speaking in very broken English.

"Yeah, give us some calamari and a bottle of shiraz please."

"Did you know what he was saying?"

"Not at all."

"Yeah, you don't get much more Italian than that, waiters that are actually *from* the homeland!"

Our tiny two-seater table is crowded with a bottle of wine, mussels and a delectable portion of black linguine with clams. I study the décor; it's a narrow restaurant with white cloth tables that run along the walls, and a painted ceiling. I watch the people in their respective conversations, hands flying up into the air, loud and boisterous—quintessential New Yorker.

And then my mind shot to her. I wondered if she had any idea. And so I prodded; the thing Jack didn't take to very well. I had seen a glimpse in Dallas but I was curious for more. I was curious as to why someone would go to the lengths he had.

"So, how long have you been married?"

The wine helped my candor. Jack flashes me a sardonic smile.

"You ask a lot of questions. Oh, about seventeen years. We met in college. I was a Finance major and she, a Political Science major. She'd always possessed strong opinions, never failing to voice them. Back then I didn't think about what effect that would have nearly twenty years later. Young and dumb."

"Wow. Did you want kids or was that kind of something she was adamant about?"

"Well what's the point in getting married? Most people want kids right?"

"Some marriages are childless. They've got less headaches too."

"True, true." Jack smirks.

"Five years passed before the kids came. I would have been happy with one, but we ended up having two.

Debra was elated. The day they were born, my life as I knew it was gone, never to return."

Debra. That must had been her name. First time I had heard him mention it.

"I don't really think about the state of my marriage. Like I said in Dallas, she just kind of does her thing and I do mine. Most important thing is that the kids are taken care of."

"But don't you think they pick up on that tension?"

"There's no tension when you don't communicate except for the necessities."

"Those few times you called me on evening walks, was that following some kind of squabble?"

Jack chuckles.

"Perhaps it was. Debra dove headfirst into those maternal inclinations, everything suddenly became about the kids. She didn't make herself up anymore. She'd just throw her hair under a ball cap. And sex became only with the lights off, and the way she wanted it. To be honest the lights off was better. It made it that much easier to imagine a more taut, polished version of a female."

To hear him speak of his wife with such disdain

was alarming but also, a stark reminder of men and their carnal proclivity. I'd seen it night after night at the club. They all wanted some hot little vixen to dote on. But they also wanted a woman to start a family with, a woman not synonymous with sexuality, but with nurturing. I didn't look at him as an asshole but more or less a human with needs that weren't being met. Of course there were two sides to every story, but the more he spoke, the more grateful I was for being on this side of the fence.

"So what brought you to the club?"

I had my own presumptions about why he had come. Vice. Freedom. Debauchery. Greed.

"I guess I yearned for something more to look at within the last few years. Does that make me a selfish asshole? Some women would argue yes."

Jack made no qualms about his self-serving persona. This is what brought him pleasure, a respite from the dry confines of home.

The waiter comes by and gives us a generous pour of wine. I grab it like it's the last supper and wait for it to numb my thoughts. I couldn't believe what I was hearing.

"Why do you stay? Sounds like it's a lost cause."

"Ha, easier said than done. When you're in my tax bracket, you keep her." The man was fucked up. A fucked up mess of a man with a lot of money.

* * *

"At 47ᵗʰ sir." The cab driver calls.

Tipping the driver, we exit a cab back to the hotel. With the Shiraz fluttering through my veins, I trot beside Jack, entering the Intercontinental lobby side-by-side, weary of any nearby colleagues.

MSNBC blares from the television and I hop onto the bed, stretching out in a pair of lacy nude panties and a tank as I flip through my NYC guidebook.

Stripping himself of his corporate echelon uniform, Jack stands in the bathroom, his tie falling to the floor. His cuff links were undone, and a glimpse of his white undershirt beckoned for a closer look. He looks hot. I pretend not to notice him.

"Come here,"

Jack crawls onto the bed, motioning himself between my legs, throwing the guidebook to the floor.

"Hey, I was reading something!"

"I don't care."

Exhaling, his heaviness traps me. I let out a sigh.

"What are you sighing about, little lady?" I could feel his breath atop me now, inching uncomfortably closer, not that he ever cared about my comfort.

"Your selfish, pompous ass."

"Ha! I love it when you call me that."

"Nothing could be closer to the truth."

Lowering his cheek to mine, he nuzzled my lips. Turning my head to the left and right, I dodged his mouth—on purpose. A hardening between his legs hungrily pressed into me.

"Don't you turn your head away from me."

"I'll turn my head all I want."

Pinning my arms above my head, our noses flirt as I laugh at his domination factor.

"Is someone getting lippy?"

"Totally." I say, biting my lip.

"You know what happens there."

"I absolutely do."

"Let me see that freckle a little closer," he says, looking down at a splay of dots on my chest. Perching himself on his knees, he drags me by the ankles to the foot of the bed. "Jack!"

Dropping his pants and shirt to the floor, his hardening is front and center in white briefs. My legs flank him on either side, and I can feel warmth envelop in my groin as I lie before him.

The reverberating sounds of the city below are drowned out as hungry hands pull my panties down to the floor. Jack tugs on my earlobe with a nibble and with two fingers, he smiles in satisfaction.

"You're so wet little girl."

"It's all your fault." My eyes roll back into my head and my body jerks all over the bed. He draws circles inside me, and then draws his fingers up, slithering my liquid on the outside of my clitoris, and then on either side of my labia. Withdrawing, his briefs fall to the floor, a sinister grin splayed across his face. He is so bad. A kind of evil warped with passion and vice. A selfish, conflicted mess of a man. And I was falling in love him. I hate him. I wanted more of him.

With one thrust, I am sent into oblivion as he fills me, his carnal lust overtaking every essence of my being. Grabbing a tuft of hair, he jerks my head upright so that my breasts point up toward the ceiling. With my legs convulsing at the pleasure, my arms reach out for him as he moves in and out. I wondered what was brewing at the very minute behind those eyes; the fact he could look into my eyes with such passion and vigor, and without an inkling of remorse. Nothing.

"Come here, I want you this way."

Flipping me onto my stomach, he drags my naked rear to the edge of the bed. With one swift motion, he cracks the top of my ass with his hand, and pushes into me from behind.

"Oh Lara," he grunts.

Grabbing a free corner of the sheets, I attempt to steady myself, but it was near impossible as his 6'5" frame held much of the control. With a swivel of his hips, he changes position, entering me from behind at a new sideway angle that sends me into heaven. I let out a wail of pleasure as a branching heat grows within me.

"Yeah, yeah, ah, ah!" I stifle my helps into a pillow.

Dizzy, I peek back at him through my legs to see the motion of his hips furiously moving back and forth into me. It was beautifully carnal. As the sensation grew deeper, I suddenly felt a pang of euphoria and with one arm, I whipped around, leaving a tiny scuff upon his stomach. Collapsing onto me, our rapid breaths relax into a labored unison as we both come.

"Come here you, don't like it when you're so far."

"But I'm not far, I'm right here in the bed."

It wasn't enough for me to be in the same bed as him. I had to be entangled with him. Two hankering arms coddle me into a slumber, and with one leg draped over him; I rest my head upon a tangle of chest hair as my pulse begins to slow.

17

Grand Central Terminal. The place smells of wrought iron and fuel, alive with a tangle of hurried people reporting to their connections. Listless school kids stand in cliques with backpacks, immersed in their iPods. Tourists stand in the middle of the clamor, wide eyed and attempting to capture the moment with their cameras.

Aside from the actual terminal stood this whole underground network of restaurants and bars. I stroll up to a place called the Magnolia bakery, scoffing at the $3.75 price tag for a tiny cupcake. But this was New York. I take two. One for me and one for Jack.

Looking up, I knew that the MetLife building was only about a block away from the Intercontinental, so I just followed the numbers, going down until I hit 48th.

The cool dusk of the evening greets me as I cover block by block back to the hotel, quietly laughing to myself as I play an imaginary exchange between my father and I in my head. "Yeah I'm walking around midtown Manhattan right now. No big deal."

* * *

"Where'd you go today? Wow, this is really good." Jack says, tearing into the cupcake.

"I went to Grand Central station."

"Oh, neat. Did you take a subway ride?"

"Negative."

"All the times I've been to the city I've never stepped foot in the place. A few movies have been shot there."

"You're stuck in that corporate utopia paradigm all day. Whose situation is worse?"

"True. Well that's why you're here."

Jack scrolls down his never-ending catalog of emails, the bright light of his phone illuminating the furrow between his brows. I pretend to look aimlessly out the window but can't help but adore this small feature of his. I loved seeing him deep in thought, so studious and methodical.

18

New York had been a blast. I found I was still in New York City mode, zipping around through Marble Beach traffic like the cabs did. We were in the south: the pace was a bit slower here.

Saturday morning. I clean the apartment that I've been absent from lately. My suitcase lies on the floor, receipts, brochures and dirty clothes lie in it. I hang my coat and scarf up. January in Florida wouldn't have me needing it so much. I place some mementos on my shelves beside my Dallas ones: a small snow globe, a tea light holder depicting the NYC skyline, and some art purchased from a street vendor. My collection was growing more diverse with each passing month, and so was my comfort level.

The days of scraping by night after night to collect

rent were gone. My credit score improved from Jack's assistance. For the first time in my life, I had more than $5,000 to my name. This dizzying arrangement—or relationship—or something that really had no name, had now become my new norm.

19

July 2012

"Suits this time?" I ask.

Cradling his head on his temple, he pries his thumbs off his eyebrows. He looks stressed. "Ah, yeah. It's gonna suck. I have to walk three blocks to Park in those."

Our room is on the tenth floor of the Waldorf-Astoria. There's one window, one very small bathroom and an even smaller closet, two queen beds, a nightstand and a desk. The New York City rooms were the simplest but also the most expensive. I looked to the key sleeve with Charters written on the first line. the next line: rate $350. *Wow, and that's the corporate rate? Damn.*

Pescatore was a quaint Italian restaurant off 2nd and 51st. A bright red awning with a fish motif adorned the outside. This being my second trip to the city, I'd treated my first time as a kind of crash course to immerse myself into the New York swing of things. This time around I felt a better acquainted but was still far from a pro.

Walk fast. Bump into people. Flag a cab down. Grab a Starbucks. Stash money in your knee-high boot. Pescatore wasn't spacious at all, small but beautifully simple, each table was adorned with a skinny vase displaying a single fresh flower, and booths were upholstered in a creamy white. Candles flickered among the hum of dinner conversation.   We take a booth, and Jack's long legs stretch beneath it. He didn't waste any time for the wine list before the waiter could promote the specials for the evening, with each of us asking for a recap due to his thick Italian accent. This was New York: people from all walks of life.

"We'll have a bottle of your best Shiraz please and some shrimp scampi please, thank you."

We break some ciabatta and make a toast. "To New York, thanks for coming."

My eyebrow shoots up. "You say that like I had a choice." I say, grinning behind my glass.

"True," His eyes dart down to the white tablecloth and

then back at me, eyes bold. "Well, you didn't. It's part of your job. To be here." I peer out the window to the flood of New Yorkers stomping by and quell my amused frustration with another sip of Shiraz. I can feel Jack's eyes tearing into me but I don't pay it any attention.

"Back in the city. Hot isn't it?"

"Eh. It's hot but not Dallas hot." I say as I tear the tail off my shrimp. They're not deveined? What the hell.

"I must say, it's nice doing a trip with you and not having to worry about work matters. But then again it's not like that ever impeded you. My obligations, that is."

He rips the tail off, pointing the fork at me, eyebrows shooting up.

"Exactly. That's why you've always been compensated. You're still working, just in another way. You're catching on. Took you awhile but you're catching on."

And then the phone. I don't think we've ever made it through one dinner without it going off. But I refrained from saying anything. I'd gotten used to him holding a fork in one hand and scrolling emails in the other while attempting to carry on conversation.

The waiter comes with our entrees. A heaping tangle of linguine tossed in a white wine sauce for me, and Jack a grilled slice of Yellowfin tuna with asparagus.

Blushing, I blink at him coquettishly through my lashes, "Happy to be here with you."

"Awe."

Jack's phone rings, cutting into this saccharine moment. I peer to his iPhone, the display reads Mark.

"What does this guy want? Hold on, let me get this."

Jack's simper fades and he heads outside, loitering in front of the restaurant for about five minutes. Watching him from the table, he smiles and laughs while his hands occasionally strike up in the air, so I know it's not some bad business news. He saunters back in and I pretend to be focused on swirling my pasta with a fork and spoon.

"That was one of my superiors. He used to live in Marsh Harbor too, got a divorce, and now he lives right here in the city. Nice huh?"

I look up from the noodles as I slurp the last one up between my lips, nodding.

"He wants me to meet him for a drink."

Deadpan. "Oh. Okay. Well, do you have to?"

"Kinda. If I don't he's going to wonder why. He's about a block up from here at a little Irish pub. You've got the hotel key right?"

"Yeah."

"Money?"

"Yes."

"Okay. Why don't you go shopping or something? Or is there something around here you can see for a bit while I go meet up with him?"

I could feel my blood boiling. I wasn't high maintenance in the least, but he'd never pulled something like this. And while I was fully capable of carrying on in New York solo, I was really enjoying this moment with him and now the ambiance was interrupted. Sigh.

With my appetite suddenly M.I.A., I try unsuccessfully to mask my frustration with the dessert menu, which I place strategically in front of my face.

"Any creme brûlée?" Quintessential Jack; oblivious to my frustration because he's mindlessly concerned with only himself.

"Yep." I snap.

"Anything for dessert madam?" The waiter asked.

"We'll have two creme brûlée and two cappuccino please. And the check."

I lost my appetite, but I didn't have the opportunity to tell him that. He'd already ordered for me. Indifferent, I crack the layer of burnt sugar with my spoon, wallowing in my cappuccino as I watch Jack devour his. Again, the phone. It was the guy.

"Jack, where ya at?" A voice beckons through the phone.

"Hey Mark, I'm coming. Just beat some foot traffic. Yeah. Sounds good, see you soon." He slips me $300 before the check even arrives.

"Okay, here's for dinner. Hold on to the rest. The bar is a block up from here. Murphy's pub. You can come there if you want, we'll just have to do James Bond. See you later." My eyes follow him as he disappears out the door. Evening was closing in now, the storefront windows glistened in oranges and golden yellows and the pavement was drenched in a kind of pink late afternoon cast. The waiter pulls me back into present time.

"Madame, how do you wish to pay?"

I pay the $150.00 tab and am off.

* * *

Murphy's was your prototypical NYC Irish pub, a

few blocks down. Stained glass motifs greet passersby's from the exterior. The place was drenched in deep mahogany tones with a swirling brown bar toting a variety of taps like Smithwicks and Guinness. There I see Jack at the bar, sitting next to Mark sharing some laughs. I glide behind them, undetected. Taking a chair about five seats down, I purposely shook the chair as I made myself comfortable, Jack's eye catching me nonchalantly.

"Hello madam, what can we get you today, a Glenfiddich's or Jameson? "The bartender greets me in a thick Irish accent.

"Oh no, Scotch will have me on the floor. Just a glass of Shiraz please."

I sip my wine, tune my ear to their conversation but only hear bits and pieces. "Work", "Spreadsheets", "Meetings" float around but I can't make any connections. Jack sends the occasional glance and I hide my smirk in the wine glass. This was hilarious. I can't believe we're actually partaking in this.

"Where's the bathroom?" I ask the bartender.

"Straight down those stairs miss."

I slide out my barstool, walking right past Jack and Mark, who cocks his head in my direction.

"Wow, did you see that broad right there Jack? They don't make him like they used to." Mark says as I slip downstairs. I chuckle. There's a woman in the next stall chatting on the phone in what sounds like Italian. I silently shake my head at the ridiculousness of it all and then a text.

*Get up here.

Ah. Jealousy? Envy? Who knows.

I come back upstairs to see him sitting alone and take a seat beside him this time, much to the bewilderment of the bartender who was visibly trying to figure out what had just happened.

"He just left. You ready to go?"

"Yeah, let me finish this."

I take one last gulp. "Thank you." I say to the now puzzled bartender. I could read that guy's mind now: weren't those two strangers fifteen minutes ago and now they're leaving together? I must pour good drinks, he might be thinking.

20

We open the door to a shadowy emptiness. The air is stagnant and smells of linen. A shard of light splinters across the floor from the window.

"That was a good act today, missy."

"Well, I've learned from the best haven't I?"

"That you have."

I jump into Jack's arms, lifting me up, I wrap my legs around him as our mouths crash into each other. I can't stop kissing him. I move to his neck and then his ear, planting little kisses, taking him in. He smells so good, robust and masculine. Eddie Bauer. Moving toward the bed, he drops me down onto the mattress, my legs hanging off the side as he pushes my pencil skirt up past my knees. Kneeling, he hungrily divides my legs, moving my panties to the side. I don't fight him. I want him. I want him now.

Jack produces small flicks of the tongue on my clitoris and then long, drawn out laps. I moan out. He then inserts two fingers, making a hook like motion that sends me out of this world. I start moving wildly, the sheets kicked up, my moaning becoming more intense. I look down at him but in the darkness I only see the crescent of his head down there.

"You're so wet."

Sighing out in desire, I struggle to get the words out as he massages me now with three fingers. "Yes. Yes, it's you."

With each hook motion, my convulsions become more pronounced. My body's moving in a kind of rhythmic back and forth motion that I don't care to control. But Jack does apparently. Taking his free hand, he suppresses my movement, clamping my leg down. With the other hand, he withdrawals his fingers, rolling the viscid consistency between his fingers, looking at it like a kid on Christmas. He sucks on his index finger.

"Mmm, you taste so good."

I lie there like a deflated effigy; my own breaths ringing in my ears. Sliding his hand under my neck, he adjusts me to the top of the bed, my head resting in the dollop of the pillows. His breaths, deep and hungry, warm my dank skin. Our noses flirt with each other as I cup his cheek. Our mouths find each other once again, and I kiss him wildly as his heavy frame finds itself between my expanding legs, and then a cry out.

"Oh…"

Pushing into me fast and hard, with one hand he pins my leg up to the headboard. It hurts but I don't care. My arms encircle him, massaging his hair, grabbing small tufts with each thrust.

"Oh, you feel good," he mutters between breaths, his neck outstretched and head pointed up toward the ceiling.

I try to speak through the thrusts. "You. Feel. Ah! Ah-maz-ing."

For a moment, the light from the window highlights a side of his face, and all I can see is a pair of emblazoned eyes burning into me. Pulling out, he releases my nearly numb leg and fashions it next to my other, pulling me toward him by my ankles.

"Come here."

Flipping me on my stomach, one hand slides under my middle, propping me upright on my knees, my face planted in the pillows. He then crashes into me, sending waves through my body. He feels the absolute best this way, and my moans become more intense and succinct. Pressing his hand down on my back, he depresses my body so my breasts are on the sheets and my rear hangs freely in the air.

"Aggghhhh." Jack lets out.

Going deeper, I whip my hand around, leaving a scratch on his belly.

"What'd I tell you about that?"

I silently smile under the guise of hair hanging over my face. While still inside me, he grabs my left hand and holds it behind my back and repeats with the other, gripping them tightly like someone under arrest. He steadies my hips with his other hand and slides me back toward him, once again pressing my back down. Then a slew of smacks come down hard on my ass. One on each cheek as my hands stay bound behind my back. I can't move. I can't do anything. Lowering his head beside mine, he speaks something almost inaudible while still thrusting.

"Is that mine?"

Between his breaths and mine, I can hardly understand him. He then bends down, grabbing a fistful of my hair, yanking my head back.

"Ah. Uh-huh."

"That's mine, huh?" His cheek nuzzling mine, his thrusts become harder and more carnal. Each one robbing me of my words as my head is held high. "Mine."

Releasing my hair, my head falls back into the pillows but my hands are still bound. I must have looked like some masochist's dream. I attempt to turn onto my back but he's not done. Sliding both arms under my midsection, he brings me to the edge of the bed so that he's standing now. My legs flanking either side of him, he pushes into me once more but this time hurls me up into the air as he thrusts, releasing me so I fall into the pillows, creating a kind of weird up and down thrusting motion. We do this one, two, three, four times as I try to catch my breath. This is a new thing. He's never done this before. But I kind of like it. It's carnal. It's hungry. It's him being controlling and powerful at his finest. This is what he wants.

21

Jack slams the alarm at 6:00 am. I blink at him through a half-comatose stare, brushing matted hair out of my face as he moseys on to the shower. The city is relatively quiet right now, but in about an hour that familiar beat of honks will begin its busy chorus once again.

"What are you going to do today?" He calls from the shower.

"Not sure yet. But I know I won't have trouble finding something."

"Wish I had that freedom. I'm going to be walking three blocks to work in this suit, dying from cardiac arrest."

Emerging from the shower, beads of water roll down his

belly. His hair a mess, I liked it spiky and disheveled; a sexy respite from his tightly kept comb game in the corporate world. He throws two ties on the bed, both similar with patterned yellow and gray squares.

"Which tie do you think is better?"

"Well they're awfully close babe, but I'd say the one on the left. More gray in it."

"Have fun today. Got a dinner with some of my guys at 7:00. Going to try and get out early. I'll text you." Kneeling down to kiss me on the forehead, I wrap my arms around him as he plants one solid kiss on my lips.

* * *

8:30 A.M. Rolling over on my side, I hit the alarm clock. The city was definitely alive now. The echo of honks bounced off the labyrinth of buildings outside, making some sound shuteye nearly impossible. Shuffling to the bathroom, I rub my eyes and nose. A stinging sensation. I turn on the light.

"What the?"

I examine myself in the mirror. A small, faint blue shadow hinted along the bridge of my nose. I tapped it. Pain. Where is that possibly from? Turning, I look at the empty bed, and a slew of memories flash by. *Oh my god. Do I really have a bruise on my nose from last night's mattress gymnastics?* Wow. Well that was a first. I couldn't wait to tell Jack that tidbit of information later.

I fashion myself on the bottom of the tub, studying the little pool of water welling up on my stomach, and I watch myself in its reflection. Tiny tributaries stream down my ribs and between my legs, disappearing into the drain.

Stepping out, I pass a brush through my hair, the length coming below my ribcage now. I really did need it cut. If I didn't have such a demanding guy in my life I would've gotten it done before I came here.

"What the—"

Passing the brush one more time through my hair, it came away again, full of auburn strands.

"You've got to be freaking kidding me."

I fan my fingers through my hair, retrieving clumps of loose, tangled strands. They fall to the floor, covering my feet. Good god, last night might as well have been a marathon boxing session. And here I was in the corner nursing my wounds. Well, there goes my first 'rough sex' audition. I'd say I came out with flying colors, with a bruised nose and clumps of hair to boot. I dab some foundation over my little shiner from last night and venture out for some breakfast.

* * *

I walk a few blocks north on 53rd, stumbling upon a place called Cafe Europa. The place was disheveled and busy but there wasn't necessarily a line. People just walked up and yelled their orders. So I followed suit in the breakfast rush.

"What ya want, doll?" The cashier shouts from behind the counter.

I order some eggs, sausage and fruit and take a seat next to the floor to ceiling window. I want to see the haphazard clamor that is New York City pedestrian traffic.

The diversity got me once again. Each table carried on in a different language than the one beside it. A Muslim woman sat next to a Jewish man sporting a frizzy beard and corkscrew sideburns. And no one felt compelled to tell each other which way is the right way and vice versa. There was tolerance. To find a demographic like this was nonexistent back in Marsh Harbor and Marble Beach.

It was definitely a hot one today, my sundress

ruffling in the warm breeze of the city. Opening maps on my iPhone, I look at midtown Manhattan. I'd seen much of this part of the city already. I wanted to discover a new borough.

I got some stares when native New Yorkers as I walked in the sticky summer heat. But mostly it was because of the distance I was walking— all the way down to Greenwich Village—some forty blocks worth. Taking Avenue of the Americas, I smile as each numbered street got smaller and smaller until I finally stood in front of Washington Square Park. I wipe the sweat from my brow, admittedly taken by the quaint beauty of it. A canopy of oak trees flank the brick pathways that wind throughout the park. Panhandlers with upside down fedoras as makeshift change deposits beg for some good graces. NYU students lie under the sun on blankets, studying. Families picnic together. Dogs chase Frisbee. Drifters with backpacks play a mellow tune on a ukulele. Contortionists perform to dazed and confused bystanders as some European tune bellows from a boom box. This kind of oasis within the concrete jungle had me smiling. If anything, it was beautiful.

22

6:00. Where had the day gone? I make my way back to Midtown and then an unexpected slice of heaven pops up right in the heart of the city: Hofbraühaus..This was Jack's kind of place; laid back, fun atmosphere. A nice aside from all those pricey dinners we do on the regular.

*At Hofbrauhaus off 3rd. Come here after work dinner.

A set of wooden stairs leads up to a boisterous accordion band, joyfully belting out tunes in German. I was already in love with the place and I hadn't even had the opportunity to say, "Ein bier bitte." Mustering up to the bar, a bright-eyed waitress hands me a menu.

"Will there just be one tonight?"

"No. There will be one more later."

"Okay, well here's our specials for tonight. Let me know if you need anything. My name's Deidra."

"Okay, can I have a Franziskaner for now?"

"A woman that knows what she wants."

"This is really cool they've got one right here in the city. Pretty sure the original is in Munich."

"Yeah, it's been open for just two years." She says, pouring me a tall glass of frothy, German goodness. I study the menu. Authentic. Everything was in German with English subtitles. I settle on the Jaegerschnitzel and spaetzle and crack open my NYC travel book.

Where was Jack? I decide to text him.

*Are you okay? It's 10:30 and haven't heard from you.

I was three beers in now and my resolve was more direct.

"Hey. I was waking up the stairs as you were texting."

I nearly jump out of my seat.

"Oh my god you scared the crap out of me!"

Typical Jack. A master of popping up, whether text or physical form.

"Hi I'll have a Sam Adams."

"Sam Adams in a German pub? You've got to broaden your horizons babe." I push my Franziskaner in front of him as he plants a kiss on my cheek. A blaring accordion rendition of A-Ha's "Take on Me" plays on and I crack a smile.

"That's mine right there."

"Uh huh," I huff as I roll my eyes.

23

"Where'd you go today?" We buzz along in the back of a cab to the Waldorf.

"I took a walk. Well, a rather long one. But a fulfilling one."

"Greenwich Village."

"Is it like Manhattan?"

"Think Sex and the City."

"That's a girl's show. I don't watch that."

Deadpan.

"Think the New York that's depicted in movies and television shows. Tree lined streets instead of towering cold, grey buildings. Wrought iron fences adorning narrow brownstones, bohemian and eclectic. Washington Square Park is over there. I'll have to take you there next time. It's beautiful."

Jack had a hard day of meetings and I nursed my now battered feet from walking

I braced myself for the 'where is that' question, and then sure enough without fail, it came.

"Where's that?" Jack asked as our cab skirted along, my eyes glued to the barrage of city lights passing too fast by us, I wanted to take them in. I wanted to take in everything while here with him. I wanted everything to just slow down a bit.

"It's down by West 8th street. South of the Flatiron district."

"You were down on 8th street today? How freaking far is that?"

"Kind of far," I smiled.

"And where's the Flatiron? What is it?"

"It's a district named for the Flatiron building, one of the most distinct architectural feats in the city, don't you know."

"You know you look like a true New Yorker—and starting to sound like one." Jack quips.

"Just watching you, how you can get around in the city so freely. You're like a natural by now. But still a nerd."

"Right. Because a nerd can hold her own in New York without having to hold someone's hand. I believe a nerd would be one who's codependent and intimidated of the city."

"Perhaps."

"If it wasn't for me, you probably wouldn't know much more of the city beyond your route to and from the office."

"True."

24

My last day in the city. Living in Florida had made my view of extreme heat quite partisan, believing northern cities couldn't possibly be as steamy as the sunshine state. But the city surprised me with how the towering buildings trapped the heat, making the stench of garbage and sewer sludge all the more pungent.

$500 lay on the nightstand for me. I'd hit the bank first and keep the rest for sightseeing. I head down 42nd to 10th and go north. The sun's punishing rays ignite my feet along the sidewalk. July in the city was no joke. The further away I got from the heartbeat of tourism in Times Square, the more I liked it. The more reticent areas of the city—the areas where no one was really elbowing each other to see—those had their own measure of intrigue.

The twenty blocks or so up to Lincoln Center along tenth was dotted with patio dining, wrought iron chairs that sat New Yorkers and tourists alike, flanked with waiters who greeted you with napkins draped over their arms. Coffee shops and pita bars stood side by side, and the aroma from cigar shops displaying Cubans tickled your nose as you walked by.

Tenth was an interesting gem in itself for having been outside the raging pilgrimage that flocks to Times Square. A tiny bead of sweat rolls down my temple.

*Where are you at, nerd?

Blushing, I text him back.

*Up by Lincoln Center.

Full well knowing that Jack had absolutely no clue as to where I was, I added the cross streets.

*65th and Broadway.

*What are you doing all the way up there?

*Seeing the city. There *is* more to do than Midtown, you know.

*Whatever nerd. Be back at hotel around 5:00. Getting out early. Figure out dinner for tonight.

And he was gone. I slip his domineering ways into my pocket and snap some photos. Even when he was trying to be kind, he still couldn't help but bark orders.

I close in on the foot of the Lincoln Center fountain. Seeing this place in the movies didn't do it justice. The place was huge; the plaza in itself echoes its 1960's birthright in design. The Metropolitan Opera House, the David Koch Theater and the David Geffen Hall all greet me as I make my way toward the dancing fountain in the center of the plaza, the focal point of the cultural arts center. The plaza was relatively dead at this time in the early afternoon, but I loved it sparse; it was though I had it to myself; no elbowing to get where I needed to.

* * *

Zahir, read the driver's ID card through the heavily fingerprinted partition. I had yet to meet one with a basic American name like Michael or John.

"Where to?"

"The Guggenheim."

"Ah, Upper East Side. Okay."

The dank scent of curry hangs in this cab and it reminds me of my maiden cab ride the first time in the city. I feel like gagging with each sharp turn and abrupt stop he makes. It was only two miles from Lincoln Center but on the opposite side of Central Park; cabbing it would be easier.

"This here is Guggenheim," says Zahir in very broken English.

I tip him $9 and step out. A peculiar smooth white stucco building that resembles something of a spaceship stands before me. Field trips of schoolchildren in matching blue shirts and Chinese tourists pose for photos stood outside the museum. The entryway was flanked with cascading flowerbeds, and a small display of local art for sale hid from the sun underneath umbrellas.

The museum's foyer was cold, white and a bit institutionalized. Signs proclaiming 'No photography' were littered all over the place. Above stood a massive glass atrium that if you stared at it long enough, brought on a kind of dizzying spell.

I take my place in line among locals and tourists speaking in a plethora of languages. To reach each gallery, you followed a cylindrical ramp pathway that wrapped around the entirety of the building until you reached the top. Or, you could opt for the elevator. But I saved that for the elderly.

Following the spiral walkway, I climb to every floor, taking in the distinct art galleries on exhibition. A myriad of styles were housed within the Guggenheim, from abstract, impressionism, photography, and mixed medium.

25

     I had become a kind of local transplanted from my own locality. I could name city streets in Dallas off the top of my head. I could flag down a cab with no avail. I could tell you the difference between the bohemian vibe of Greenwich Village and the structured business acumen of Manhattan.

     A heavily wooded area stood across the street, an archaic stonewall enclosing it from the rest of 5th Avenue. That must be Central Park. My eyes scan the Jackie Onassis reservoir. Apartment buildings of New York's past—the San Remo and Dakota— stood on the other side like statuesque royalty.

*You headed back? Where are you?

*Guggenheim. Upper East Side.

*Where?

Smiling, I expected this much. Because it was out of his familiar crutch of Midtown.

*The Guggenheim. One of the most popular art museums in the city.

*Don't know. You got dinner plans figured out yet?

I roll my eyes.

*You're interrupting my Central Park moment.

*I thought you were at some Guggenheim place.

*I am! It sits across the street from the park.

*Well, you just get all over don't you? Just make sure you're back around 5:30 for dinner.

* Whatever.

* * *

Stepping out of the museum, a lanky, ash-blonde man with an unshaven beard saunters to me.

"Hello ma'am, how are you this afternoon?"

"I'm a little hot, but well. And you? Are these your works here?" The sun was blinding today. I point to a display of ink and paint works that capture every borough of the city. His work held a consistent whimsical style, with crooked lines and colors fused together to give the city a fun, illustrated beat.

"I have a special today, two 8x10 autographed prints for $40 or one for $25."

While any artist could appreciate a compliment, let's face it: the man was in business. And if he lived here in New York, he definitely had to make some kind of living, and a lucrative one at that. Scrolling his display, I'm especially taken with one of the Flatiron, I admired its imperfect architectural shape, and its reputation as a timeless landmark of New York City.

"I'll take this one."

"Is that all ma'am? We have quite a collection here. This your first time to the city?"

"Oh, no. I've been here before."

"A woman who likes to travel. Nice."

And then the first drop hit my arm. Rain. An ominous shelf of dark gray clouds hung in the distance. I was uptown sans umbrella. Great.

"I think that will be all for today, but maybe next time, thanks!"

I begin walking with one arm shot up in the air for a cab. Joggers sprint to the nearest cover in the park. Tourists toting cameras and visors scatter into various directions. And then the deluge came. I take cover under a tree and watch the artist I'd just bought from scurry to save his art.

The Guggenheim was right across the street but in the few minutes it would take to get there, my art would be ruined indefinitely, not to mention other things, like my hair. And I had dinner in one hour. *Fuck.* I wondered what Jack was doing. He hated being late especially when he was hungry. He got that "hangry" problem. Angry drops of rain stabbed the air, awakening a number of mosquitoes.

I stand there under my small canopy of pine needles and look around. A couple speaking in a foreign language stands beside me. A Hispanic man with a handlebar mustache behind me. Two boys with skateboards. A gang of strangers under one common tree in the concrete jungle. I check my phone. Nothing. Perhaps he was still in a meeting.

"Well, what a day right?" I say aloud.

The foreign couple laughs and nods in agreement.

"Yeah, this our first time to New York. The weather is like back home."

They were both blonde and blue eyed, and spoke in decent English, but not complete polished diction.

"Where are you guys from?"

"Norway."

I smiled at this small revelation.

"Really? I was there a few years back. In a city called Stavanger. That was my first time out of the country."

The two of them lit up like kids at Christmas.

"Wow. Most Americans don't even know about Norway, let alone a city like Stavanger."

"Yes, it was beautiful. I loved it. Also the first time I had shrimp with mayonnaise to boot!"

The man speaks Norwegian to his girlfriend, and then English back to me.

"We are from near Oslo."

"Nice. What do you guys think of the city?"

"Well, it's nice, but not today!" They both laugh in

unison. I enjoyed watching them; two people who seemingly couldn't take their eyes off one another. I knew that kind of amorous look. I had shared that very one with Jack for a while now, across state lines and a blur of airports.

Lightning branches across the sky and a loud clap of thunder pierces my ears. Across the street, the Guggenheim was no longer visible in the pelting rain. I swat at the nape of my neck. The mosquitoes were starting to bite. I had to make a run for it.

The rain wasn't tapering off but I had to get back to the hotel. Wrapping my art tight, I say goodbye to my fellow tree huddlers and sprint across 5th. *Good day to be without an umbrella.* Skipping along a puddle-stricken sidewalk, I continue shooting my arm up in the air. Not a taxi in sight. I had never seen the streets so uncomfortably empty like this before, literally robbed of those yellow blurbs.

Another sheet of rain began to beat the pavement and I take cover under a hotel awning with a few others. An elderly woman stands beside me, her hair tucked under one of those plastic rain bonnets. Her feet had vanished under the unrelenting rainwater.

"Well this is odd. First time to the city where I can't find a cab." I say aloud, hoping someone would provide an answer.

"No, this is common for this time of the day." An Indian man says behind me.

"Well, what time is it?"

"It's around 4:30. That is shift change."

26

My luck in getting a cab was vanquishing and I was already going to be late to dinner. How much worse could it really get? I could get a little more drenched than I already was. So let's try another street and try my cab luck. Sloshing through puddle after puddle, I wind up on Madison Ave, passing by the quaint boutiques with designer duds on even more pretentious-looking mannequins.

My hair sopping wet, I flick one heavy strand out of my face as I stand on the crest of a hill, looking down to oncoming traffic. Mascara stings my eyes as I wipe droplets from my face. One, two, four, six, ten cars speed by, and not one of them a cab.

"Unfuckingbelievable!" I cry out.

* * *

"Looking for a cab too?" A male voice calls. Turning around, two men, middle-aged, stood in grey suits with briefcases.

"That I am, and having terrible luck with it!"

"Yeah, this time of day sometimes it can be impossible."

Oh no. I didn't like that word. I couldn't have impossible. Not right now. Couldn't have that. I needed a *possible* right now.

"Where are you trying to get to?"

"The Waldorf."

"Oh man off Park?"

"Yes. That's my hotel."

"Oh. The way you said it, I didn't think you were a tourist. Did you, Mike?"

"No, no not at all. You must know your way around the city well."

"Perhaps. I've been here a handful of times."

"Oh yeah? Just by yourself or—"

"No, with my boyfriend. He has work up here."

Boyfriend. Well Jack wasn't a boyfriend. In fact I wasn't really sure what he was. It just was what it was.

"Cool. What does your boyfriend do?"

"Charters enterprises."

"Oh yeah. Their headquarters are off Park right?"

"Yes."

"Well more power to him. I know how banking goes. Does he drink a lot?" The two men chuckle.

"Actually, yes. It's rare if he doesn't have some alcoholic beverage after a long twelve hour day." I smile at their accuracy.

"I used to work in banking. Bank of America to be exact. I think I sprouted a few premature grays during my stint there." said Mike.

"I'm Pete by the way."

"Lara."

"Ah, my daughter's name. You want to see a picture?"

"Sure." I wait as Mike fans through his iPhone album, producing a photo of a twilight-blonde toddler with deep blue eyes.

"Oh, she's beautiful. That's cool you named her Lara. I think I've met one or two girls thus far with my name."

"Yes it's a rare one. But her mother and I liked it." Gushing over his daughter, he sticks the phone into his back pocket.

"Taxi! Taxi!" Peter calls out to the solo yellow blurb of glory that comes speeding toward us. *Hallelujah, fuck.* We squirm into the backseat like sardines, wet, uncomfortable and stinky.

"Can all three of us fit in?" Peter asks.

And I'm just worried about smelling up this cab.

27

"Where on Earth were you?" Jack scoffs as he watches me peel off my soaked garments.

"Don't start with me." I step into the shower and then begin my tirade.

"Caught in a downpour on the Upper East Side without an umbrella and attempting to flag a cab down during what I had just learned was an apparent shift change! How do cabs in NYC even have that? Isn't the demand too high? I mean, how do they just go M.I.A? Oh, by the way I have no clue what we're doing for dinner arrangements tonight."

"Are your hands flying in the air?"

"Possibly. Maybe. Okay yes."

* * *

We had done something aside from our culinary merry-go-round of steak and lobster and Italian and went for some New York City Chinese. It was superb to say the least, and Jack's loosened belt loop illustrated that.

"Come on! We have to do this. It's our last night here in the city and all you ever see is those drab office walls."

We walk along Fifth Avenue to 50th up to Rockefeller Center, hand in hand.

* * *

"Wow, look at this place." Jack's head cocked all the way back as he took in the enormity of Rockefeller. He had been to New York more times than I but here I was in a sense, guiding him around tourist haunts.

"And there's Radio City. Wow." He points to the windows.

What was this childlike innocence and what had it done with my conflicted, controlling man? We were sixty-nine floors up, together in the breezy embrace of the night sky.

"There's Times Square. You can't miss it, all the lights." Jack pointed.

A glass wall separated us from what was on the other side: death. Apparently the architects knew that there would be squalls of tourists here all vying for the perfect photo op. I appreciated their mindfulness in constructing the glass and not some netted framework.

"And there's the Empire. I've never been up in that one yet."

"Look, way down there. That's where the Twin Towers used to be." We move to the other side. A massive black mass stands in the middle of the expansive night view.

"That must be Central Park."

"Yup."

The city beamed below but I found myself more transfixed in the view of what stood beside me. I study the way his mouth curls into two puckered corners, the tiny furrows escorting those tired eyes. To see him happy for once— not consumed with work, not checking his phone, not replying to emails—but rather just enjoying a solitary moment with the city.

At that moment, standing in the dark of night with him, the few inches that stood between us are obstructing; I couldn't get close enough. Those towering shoulders draw me in close.

"Pretty cool ain't it? Were not in Marsh Harbor anymore."

"It's beautiful."

"You wanna go for a drink?"

"Sure. Some champagne would be nice."

28

A bottle of Möet sits in an ice bucket on the nightstand. Jack is on top of me, peeling my clothes off. Well at least I didn't smell like the dank scent of body odor and rain from earlier today.

"I want this off." I don't dare test him. Peeling my shirt up over my head, a pile of slacks, lacy boy shorts, a bra and Cole Haan socks quickly follow. Lying there naked, he scoops me up and we move to the bathroom.

"Where are we going?" I ask, clinging to him like a shaking leaf.

He turns the water on; a steamy stream greets us as we hop in. The pool of hot water on the bottom massages my toes, sore from getting caught in that retched rainstorm earlier. Jack's towering stature obscures the water from hitting me, goose bumps paint my skin and I begin to shiver.

"I want you," he whispers, moving toward me, those icy blue depths potent.

His hairy paunch nudges me into the corner of the shower, my back pressed against the tiled porcelain. I wrap my arms around his high shoulders and taste him as he dives into my mouth. I can't hide my smile as I cup his face, kissing him achingly. I want him too. His fingers trace from my neck down to my stomach, drawing that familiar tracing pattern he's done before. The stream of warm water trickles down my skin between our mashed bodies, warming the both of us. With his fingers encircling my pudendum, he gently inserts one. My knees suddenly feel weak and I moan aloud, my breath heightened. He revels in my response.

"Hmmm,"

Lifting me up by the thighs, he suspends me against the cold porcelain, our breaths intermingle in a melodic lust. I throw my head back in desire as I feel him take me, pushing me harder against the wall. My legs interlocked around him, he feels so good, so carnal, so hungry, and incessantly selfish. The beat of the water trickles into my mouth and my eyes roll back, an innocuous vertigo setting in. With each rhythmic thrust he pushes me harder and harder against the porcelain. I let out a wail, stabbing his back with my nails, as I come.

"Oh my god Jack. Oh my god. Wow."

"Bad girl. What did I tell you about scratching?"
Grabbing me by the hair, I steady myself against him as
I slide down the wall.

My head is jerked back down directly in front of him
now, meeting his eyes. Those stoic depths; those
conflicted, ravenous, beautiful depths flash me a
sardonic smile.

"You won't scratch me again will you?" He plasters my
one hand against the porcelain, while still holding that
transfixing gaze.

"No. No I won't."

"Look at me." He demands. I'm immediately taken back
to that private room where I met him, where he was so
adamant about eye contact.

"Good girl."

Diving into my mouth, I close my eyes and cup his face
as he takes me once more, pushing into me as I
squinting my eyes, my chest pumping out. My legs like
jelly as we hold each other under the patter of water.

29

I was cooking up one of my favorite culinary delights, stuffed mushrooms, when the phone rang.

"Hey, what are you up to?" It was Jack, taking an evening neighborhood walk. He took these more often lately. He'd hinted in Dallas that these were usually in light of some blowout at home.

"Cooking; something you're unacquainted with."

"You always get sassy when you're far away you know. It's hot outside," he says between breaths. "New York was pretty hot huh?" "Yeah I was totally *not* jealous of you beating the pavement in those Jos A. Banks suits."

My face turns red as I let out a chuckle.

"You know you should just move closer."

"Um, I have to work."

I was saying this like I really worked a great deal anymore. Both of us knew that to be an empty statement, with this past year and a half marking my greatest absence at work.

"What do you work now, one day a week maybe?"

"Kind of."

* * *

The running joke of all the girls in my business was that they were all in some capacity, in nursing school. Guys would make disparaging jokes about where the money went: "Oh I just helped some stripper through nursing school!"

The truth was, you couldn't put all of us under one umbrella. Some girls were in school while some were not. Some had drug problems and some saved their money. Some were supporting kids. Some supported boyfriends. Others even had pimps where they were conditioned into thinking they served as a "money

manager" of sorts. We were all different. But you
learned in time to take the remarks with a grain of salt,
to let your perseverance be the final slap in the face to
the dissenters.

30

August 2012

Reports of financial woes from my fellow dancers reminded me that I wasn't missing much more than $100-150 a night and the occasional request to come back to some lonely guy's hotel room.

A pang of guilt festered within me. While they struggled, here I was perusing the streets of New York and Dallas, eating at five star restaurants and crashing in posh hotels. But I had asked for none of this. I had stopped asking why months ago. The question of why had left my brain as I realized there was no making sense of it. This was just how it was.

I began to shift my focus, questioning things that culminated my monotony. What was I doing in Marble

Beach anymore? I was constantly up in Marsh Harbor in a barrage of coffee houses and airports. Nothing was keeping me here anymore, aside from the occasional white envelope in the mailbox from Jack. I found myself at the beach every weekend, drinking in the sun as I stared blankly at the ocean, silently wishing for it to give me some semblance of understanding.

* * *

Admittedly I had floundered in finding my path. Growing up, I recall my dad pushing for something in healthcare. "People always get sick," he'd repeated. "The demand is there!"

I had had a brief stint as a Phlebotomy student a few years back. And while body physiology was interesting, I found that my passion was not in it and just shy of seven months of graduating, I subsequently dropped out. What ensued were a few years of attempting to find myself. I went to Zurich for a week right before I met Jack, visiting friends, not wallowing but more or less displacing myself out of my comfort zone so as to gain some introspection with my current state of life.

The one thing that had always come naturally to me was writing. From the time I was little I had written and illustrated my tales, my family proudly serving as my audience, especially on holidays when there were more ears. In middle and high school I had a pile of diaries, some of them filled to the brim with that kind of teenage angst that included a yearning for freedom, the pain of unrequited love and the curiosities of sex and boys.

I begin searching for universities in Marsh Harbor. And Jack is more than helpful.

"Did you check out Marsh Harbor University? Or how about Coral Cove College?"

I always found myself looking at the cost per credit hour.

"Yes and they were quite pricey. Upwards of $300 plus a credit hour."

"No good. Keep looking."

* * *

I stare at the financial aid worksheet, smirking at the questions. The drive up here had taken an hour and a half, but it wasn't like I wasn't acquainted with that or anything. Reminiscing to that conversation I'd had months before where I outlined all my expenses, it had all come full circle as I stared at these questions, all tied together by one common denominator: Jack.

Question 1. "Who if anyone supported you in any way for the calendar year of 2012?"

Question 2. "Did you receive any monetary gifts for the calendar year of 2012?"

Question 3. "How were you able to meet living expenses for the calendar year of 2012?"

Scoffing as I scribbled a bullshit answer for each question, I full well knew I had no need for the aid. When I talked to Jack about student loans and grants for the impending fall semester, Jack quieted the idea by simply saying, "Discover it." With his help, I had condensed my credit cards over the past year and a half to just one, my Discover. Evident in its scratches and a faded signature, it had heavy employment from all of my travel expenses.

Having floundered in finding a path for college, I held a strict stance that CCF would be the place where I'd walk across that graduation stage. Transferring in with seventy-five credit hours from previous academic work, I was at junior status. All it would take is two short years for a Bachelor's in English.

"Miss Arbour, the university will contact you about your financial aid award within the next two to three weeks."

The associate says as I turn in my eligibility paperwork.

"Thank you and welcome to the Coastal College of Florida."

Smiling, I peer down at my brand new student ID, complete with a most awkward grin that put my license picture to shame.

31

"Well I don't care about it helping you. I care about it helping me. These on campus classes don't help my travel schedule as you know." Jack and I sit in Starbucks with my new student packet from CCF. In it, he's going over my cost per credit, school schedule and book list.

"Oh yes, how could I forget. Jack has rendered himself incapable of traveling solo. Well let me tell you something: some of us would like to graduate sometime soon." I snarl.

Taking a sip of his coffee, his eyes tear into me.

"And that's fine. I want you to graduate too. That just means you're going have to look at your professors' syllabi and see the attendance policy. How many days you can miss before a it cuts into your grade?"

"Would you like to write me a hall pass?"

He chuckles between sips. "Ha, I ain't writing you nothing. You're just expected to be there. That is all."

"So you're transferring in as a junior. Good stuff."

I beam ear to ear.

"Well, we need to find you an apartment then. Get looking."

32

"Any luck today?"

Taking a sip from my mocha, I smile. We're sitting in our usual Starbucks, a table away from the revolving door of java seekers.

Reaching into my purse, I produce the quote given to me today, including the financial breakdown of expenses. "Looks good. Nice place?" Jack asks.

He didn't say anything about the rent. At $700, it was two hundred dollars more than my Marble Beach place was.

"Yeah, nicest I've seen yet in the past month."

"Oh, it says here it's not vacant until September 21st?" He said pointing to the brochure.

"Yeah, sucks but, I'm not going to stress over it. I'll just have to make the commute a few times a week to school."

"How many days do you have class?"

"Just Wednesdays and Thursdays, and then my online class."

"Too bad you couldn't pickup more online classes."

"Yeah, would've helped." "Hold your purse out."

I did as I was told, holding it open discreetly under the small table.

"There. I gotta run. I'll call you."

"Thanks for the coffee." I roll my eyes as I walk to my car. I hated these "cash and dash" exits he pulled sometimes.

I'm not too far down the highway before the phone rings.

"Okay, there's $1,600 there. Pay your car, rent, and then I want $500 put on the Discover. Whatever's left is walk around for you."

"Okay."

* * *

My first day of classes at the Coastal College of Florida. Last week I had purchased my books, all $450 worth. I had received $1,200 in grant money and the rest would be paid out of pocket. The campus was situated on acres of wetland and stood less than ten miles from the ocean. Marsh Harbor's location of forty-five minutes from the Georgia border predisposed me to being in the company of professors and students who shared that southern drawl, going out of their way to be nice, saying excuse me and holding doors open for you. I think this was more aptly known as southern hospitality?   As I had transferred in as a junior, most of my core classes were done and out of the way. Many of my classes were electives; the one I looked forward to most being Fiction and Non-fiction Creative Writing workshop, where you sat in a circle and annotated the writing pieces of classmates. My first semester I had signed up for nine credit hours, or three classes: Wednesdays and Thursdays from 6:00-8:45 pm and the other online—all to appease Jack's travel schedule. Well, let's face it: I could fly back from New York City and go straight to class.

I pull out of CCF's campus, I head south back down to Marble Beach. I would do the hour and a half drive two days a week for the next three weeks, until my new apartment here was ready in September.

* * *

"How much is the bill?" Jack asks over the phone on my ride home.

"Uh, $2,851 for the semester. But grant money covered $1,200."

"Ah, not bad, so we owe about $1,600 and some change."

I liked how he spoke of my finances in the context of we—like we were some kind of team. But I reminded myself this is how he was. Don't question it, just roll with it.

"Okay; when's it due?"

"They offer a payment plan, but it's a half and half plan. There are no increments less than that. I thought that was pretty unforgiving."

"You didn't answer the question; when is it due?"

I roll my eyes.

"August 26th, as in next week. They don't waste any time."

"Okay. Discover it. We'll meet for coffee later this week."

* * *

That night, I sit staring at my computer screen, surrounded by textbooks. I read through the generous list of fees accrued from CCF: athletic service fee. Counseling fee. Guidance fee. Student services fee. Technology fee. Some of these fees I wasn't even using, but they were rolled in there. The list was staggering. Surely I couldn't afford this school without Jack. But it's not like it stopped there. Surely I couldn't afford much of anything without him. And while I realized any other girl would be eating this lifestyle up, I still had my reservations. I hated feeling like I needed somebody but then I also didn't mind it either. What was the alternative? The daily newsfeeds that detailed the struggles of jobless Americans to make ends meet and skyrocketing national debt? I could be a part of that statistic. I examined my own situation and despite its strange and unconventional nature, was somewhat grateful.

33

My first week in my new apartment has me toiled. I keep on top of my homework between boxes, bubble wrap and Jack's incessant phone calls. Our conversations grow rather long in the mornings; that's how I can tell he misses me. The sheer excitement in my newly declared proximity to him likely had him stewing like a kid at Christmas. I still wasn't sure exactly where he lives, but we now shared the same zip code. I refrained from asking when he'd come over. I knew it was only a matter of time. The man was all about getting what he wanted and hated to be refused. My apartment resembles that of an Ikea catalog, with eclectic patterns and bold colors. I had retracted the stale mini blinds on the living room window that had greeted me upon move-in, replacing them with striking lime green and blue curtains. An Ikea recliner sits simply along the window beside the fireplace, and a love seat upholstered in a whimsical fuchsia floral pattern hugs the opposite wall, beneath picture ledges that display travel mementos. A 24x36-framed picture of a New York City map sits upon the fireplace ledge, nestled by two potted plants. I was on the third floor here, but I liked being on top. The cathedral ceilings in the living room and bedroom made for a spacious feeling.

* * *

"Hello?"

"What are you doing?"

"Sleeping, what do you think?"

I squint at the time through eyes half shut.

"Really? At 5:30 you're calling?"

"Yep. We start early around here. Well get up because I'm getting off your exit."

My eyes widened as I flip over on my stomach. "What? Why?"

"Giving you cash for the Discover. We gotta make a

dent in the fall tuition."

"Alright."

"Get up. Be there in two minutes."

I like how he just shows up more or less unannounced, with a blatant disregard for the fact that maybe I was tired, or didn't want him to see me like this. I smack down my inner girl as I wipe the sleep from my eyes and light a citrus candle.

"Well you weren't lying about being close were you?" I open the door to see Jack in gym clothes.

"Gym clothes? Where do you get the energy for the gym this early?"

"No. It's just my out. When I leave the house everyone's asleep anyway."

He wraps me in his arms and we stand awkwardly in the middle of my dining room among boxes and bubble wrap. I stand on my tiptoes, meeting his lips for a kiss, that familiar scent of nearly two years enraptures me, a scent of fresh laundry and Eddie Bauer. It isn't long until I feel a bump, and I come back down on the soles of my feet.

"Hmmm."

"Your fault."

"What else is new?"

Fishing in his pockets, he sets a butterfly clipped stack of money on the counter. Another clip to add to my growing collection in the junk drawer.

Somewhere in this early morning daze, I feel almost drunk. I can't believe he's in my apartment. *Holy crap, how did we get here?*

"There's $700 here. Go to the bank today, deposit this and pay off the moving costs. And here's another $200 for walk around, alright?"

"Well as if I have a choice in the matter other than to nod and oblige."

"You're learning. Alright, I have to go; got a call with Singapore at 7:00. Have a good day at school."

* * *

I saunter out to the balcony. I find myself out here often, mostly at night. My growing collection of Peonies, Kalanchoe and Petunias border the edge in terra cotta pots, their floral limbs bent toward the sun.

My windows have a clear view of a small meandering lake, which was the apartment complex's namesake: Lake Coral. Only there was no coral—well, whatever. Some of these tropical Florida complex names had me gawking at what the developers were thinking at the time.

A gang of twelve Canadian geese swims freely there. I'd see them at night sometimes; they were quite talkative, their cackling rousing me from sleep. I hadn't yet met my neighbors but part of that was my own standoffishness. I preferred to live in my secluded world of Jack and I, where our indulgences roamed freely without abandon.

* * *

Nearly two years later and I still hadn't a clue where Jack called home. Geographically, I knew he was around a mere ten miles or so from my place, just from the clues he had provided. This proximity had me doing a tug of war between happiness and trepidation. While I didn't expect him to be coming over for coffee, being closer did allow for more time together.

But I knew his methodical nature all too well. He would creep in and out at the crack of dawn, before the buzz of hurried early morning traffic, slapping me senseless with his charm and then leave, leaving me in a perpetual state of bliss for the rest of the day. Something that had remained unchanged all this time.

* * *

I flip some zucchini noodles in a pan as a home improvement show plays on. I rarely watched television, most days it was just to have something to buffer the silence. Laundry rolls on and I browse the difference between APA to MLA citation for a short paper due later in the week.

"Hit the bank today?"

"Of course."

"So moving expenses paid?"

"That would imply that."

"Smart ass. Don't make me come over there. You're closer now."

"Oh, I am shaking with fear."

"How was school? Meet any boys?" Jack pokes through the phone. He liked to entertain the prospect that I could meet single, eligible men while full well knowing I had zero interest.

"Oh yes. Loads. Couldn't keep them at bay."

"It's probably 'cause you were prancing around, being all hot in that New Balance. *My* New Balance."

Jack was a fan of my gym clothes. Who was I kidding; he'd take me in a brown potato sack.

"Someone's blushing."

"How do you know this? God, you're so weird! How is it you can just see my reaction when you're not even here?"

"I'm observant."

I imagine those eyes tearing into me, as they were oh so good at doing.

"You take being observant to a whole other level, my friend."

"I just simply asked if there were any boys looking at you at school today."

"Why do you care?"

"I don't know." Jack says coyly.

"Someone obviously hasn't overcome their self-deprecating ways yet. That much we know."

"Whatever. Hey listen, I'm pulling in. Text me account balances. Talk to you in the morning."

"Looking forward." I sneer through my teeth.

I take my dinner to the table and stare blankly at my new apartment. Almost everything in here rode on his dollar. I barely worked anymore. The place was $700 a month, could I afford that and everything else? Perhaps. But I'd have to break my back every night at the club, sashaying in that smoke filled haze for some salivating customer.

I walk out to the balcony. It was a clear night, the moon's reflection cut up by the paths of swimming geese. What a life. Fly. Swim. Mate. No cares in the world. Were they happy? My mind shot back to the days of self- sufficiency. The concept of independence had become so faded lately; a kind of ascribed purgatory had characterized my life. I hadn't paid my own rent or car in god knows when. Underneath his gratuity was a man who didn't like to be refused. In the beginning, I was too stubborn to accept Jack's money. My fierce independent nature saw his need to support as a way to put me under his thumb and at his beckon call. Had that already happened?

34

December 2012

Since it was only a 3.5-hour drive, we had driven down to Lauderdale for some conference Jack had to attend. It was a happy diversion from the usual airports and rental car routine I'd damn near perfected all this time. Jack drove his car down and put me in a rental to avoid throwing more miles on my already hefty 97,000-odometer reading. South Florida was the real Florida—the quintessential Florida depicted in travel guides, billboards and commercials that evoked a tropical paradise.

Cruising down a palmetto lined Federal highway

near the Boca Raton and Pompano border, I study the architecture of the buildings as I trail behind Jack. Villas in pastel pinks, yellows, and greens caught that tropical, jovial holiday essence that became more pronounced the closer you got to Miami.

While I could have served as my own tour guide as I did on past trips, my perfectionist academic nature found me front and center in front of my laptop writing papers while Jack was at work. It didn't matter that I had finals this week. Oh no. Nope. I suppose my own selfish nature wanted me to do both: homework and a small getaway. It's not like I'd never been to the Ft. Lauderdale area before. So this trip I treated the daytime like work: at night we'd go out to dinner. No biggie.

* * *

"So did you find anything good for dinner?"

"Yeah I kind of have a craving for Italian. Found a place not far from here in Boca."

Coming out in tan dress slacks and his shirt from work that day, he was ready.

"How are your finals coming along?"

"Not bad. I've only got five pages left on the one and ten

to go on the other. I'll make it happen."

"Okay. I'm going downstairs first. There are a lot of people staying in this hotel for the conference. I'm going to try and slip out without being seen. Meet me at the car when I text you."

"Okay babe. See you down there."

*Got caught. Got to have a quick drink with this guy.

Dammit. I slump down on the bed. Would it always be this way? Waiting on him? I move toward the window. Resting my head against the glass, I gaze down to the buzz of traffic below. Oh, but how it could be much worse. I thought about the girls. I could be one of them right now; scrounging for money in an otherwise tight-pocketed, recession ravaged crowd. But I was here. In another hotel room, in another city, about to have another dinner with my gloriously complicated, impossible, and affectionately demanding man.

"Hot dress." Jack eyes me as I climb into his car. We meet across the street at a shopping plaza, parking my rental there. Blushing, I roll my eyes as I paint a shade of peach on my lips. I'd donned a strapless floral number for tonight, sweeping my hair up in a loose bun off to the side, a few strands tickling the nape of my neck.

"Man, just as I made the corner to head to the parking

deck that guy saw me. And I couldn't get out of it; he's one of my superiors."

"Corporate utopia." I mutter.

"So what'd you get me for dinner tonight?"

"There's this place called Ocean's Prime. They've got surf and turf, but it's not limited to just that. You have to get on 95 north." I open maps on my phone. We were both repeat offenders of texting and driving, emailing and driving, bill paying and driving. My bill paying and driving had definitely increased since I met him, given his demands on getting payments done when *he* wanted them.

* * *

Cathedral ceilings and mahogany wood floors greet us in an open air dining area, the ocean simmering off in the distance.

"You should go say hi over to your twelve o'clock." Jack says.

"My what?"

"Turn around."

Two men sit at the bar, breaking their necks.

"Yeah and?"

"They're looking at you."

"And this is something new?"

"No, just saying maybe you should say hi."

"Will you stop with your self-deprecation? If you don't want people looking maybe you should trade me in for a plain Jane model."

I had to admit, Jack's apparent jealous streak had me laughing inside. That sort of thing probably didn't happen much back on the homefront.

"Just teasing you, god."

"Uh huh, sure you are." We take our seats at a table, the menus are held down by tea lights due to the ocean breeze.

"Shrimp scampi over angel hair looks good," Jack said, studying the menu. A trio of men in palm print shirts play a ukulele rendition of Sinatra's "You go to my head." I stare at the menu, cracking a smile of the sheer irony. *This* song of all his songs.

You go to my head And you linger like a haunting

refrain

And I find you spinning round in my brain

Like the bubbles in a glass of champagne

"Hey. What do want?" Didn't take long for Jack to drag me out of that dream.

"Huh?"

"Clams?"

"Yeah, yeah. Sounds appetizing."

"We'll have the littleneck clams to start," Jack points to the menu. "And a bottle of this Shiraz here, thanks."

I looked down at the Shiraz he ordered. $100 a bottle. Almost two years of gallivants and the sight of our hefty dinner bills still made me quiver. Not sure why—it wasn't like I was paying.

"Good choice on the restaurant. Salute."

"So what else is around here?"

"Well there's some pretty good hotel bars that I found browsing the locals guide in the room. You just have to follow this embankment here."

I point to a brick promenade lining the patio of the restaurant. "But really if you walk along this promenade here, there's a lot of open bars and grilles."

"Cool, we'll have to check some out later."

"Your dinner sir," our waiter arrives with Jack's meal, an impressive slab of halibut with a lemon cream sauce, red skinned mashed potatoes and vegetables. "And you, madam."

"Nice. That's not something you can make at home huh?"

I tried not to order things out that I could easily whip up in my own kitchen, so I opted for Linguine con le vongole.

"I'm getting moved."

"Moved? As in, a new position?"

"Yeah, instead of covering all of North America and Asia Pacific, I'll be global for Charters."

The tiny seafood fork slips from my fingers on to the table.

"Oh? Wow."

"Yeah, Jack shifts in his seat, a blasé look cast across his face as he pushes the last of his halibut around on the plate. While he was classically hard to read, his reservations this time were rather clear.

"And are you happy with this promotion?"

"Well, I don't exactly have a choice in the matter."

"What? How can you not have a choice? Can't you opt to take the offer or refuse it?"

"Perhaps in other companies, but in the banking world, it's a little different."

"How was that received on the home front?"

"Haven't told anybody yet. Just you."

While I was flattered, I silently wondered what held him back from announcing the news with her.

"Well it's not like you're gonna be able to fly back from Singapore for a the kids' games if you have to."

"True, true."

"Do you have a tinge of regret for that?"

"No, not really. I mean as far as the kids, they've never known any different." I go back to work on the clams, twirling them in with the linguine.

"If I can make it through the next five years maybe I can retire and save what's left of my hair at the end."

"Yes it's quite possible you might come out with more wisdom highlights within the next few years."

Snickering, I rub his forearm as he gazes out to the darkening ocean.

"May I take your plate? Any dessert or coffee tonight?" The waiter asks.

"I'm good."

"Yes, you have any creme brûlée?"

Interjecting was something of a perfected science for him.

"Jack, I'm not hungry. Not much more will fit into this dress."

The waiter hovers over us, eyes darting back and forth between our exchange.

"Uh, we'll l have the creme brûlée and also a slice of key lime. And two coffees with cream."

"Well I'm glad to see my opinion mattered with regard to dessert."

"Has your opinion ever mattered?"

"Ah yes, that's right; what on Earth was I thinking?"

I crack the top of the creme brûlée with a spoon.
Steadying a dollop on my spoon, I lick it.

"You gotta stop doing that."

"What?"

"Nothing, just the way you—"

"Oh god, really right now?" "Yes really."

"Story of my life."

"This is your life. And I control it."

35

March 2013

Jack wasn't particularly looking forward to this trip, as it invoked the darker side of corporate leadership: firing some employees and breaking the news of thinner bonuses.

"Yep, a few more weeks until doomsday. Not looking forward. I hate St. Louis."

While I was in the dark as to what lie ahead for him here, I presume the vibe would be different from previous trips.

"Yes, but you've got much happiness to look forward to in that hotel room by the end of the day."

"True statement, true statement." cracking a smile.

St. Louis stood alone from other trips, as it was the first one in which we took separate planes. Marsh Harbor didn't offer a direct to St. Louis, but Orlando did. So I drove two hours down to MCO to fly out of there. Jack's route out of Marsh Harbor involved a layover in Atlanta en route to St. Louis. I would arrive first, so I'd pick him up at Lambert-St. Louis.

* * *

I meander through Lambert airport to the rental car counter. My years of traveling with Jack had polished my airport skills from novice to varsity.

We were staying in a relatively obscure town about forty-five minutes outside of St. Louis called O'Fallon. In the cast of this sullen spring day, the town didn't seem to boast much aside from rolling brown pastures with skeletal trees and battered silos. This trip would be a short one, a day and a half to see things. We were staying at the Beechwood—not exactly the gem hotels of New York, but it sufficed. It was a very basic room with very basic amenities. But I didn't much care; I just wanted to see Jack in a few hours. I report right to my room and pop open my laptop to finish an assignment due for tomorrow night's class. This was it: my last year in college. An assignment here, an assignment there: in a random city, a random airport, a random plane and some random hotel room. How I'd managed to pull near perfect grades all this semester and the last while gaining some serious frequent flyer miles was beyond me.

I remember one time in New York, taking a psychology quiz on a rainy night at a Manhattan Starbucks. With Jack tied up in a dinner with colleagues, I sat there amidst the glow of my laptop, looking out the window between the red, green and blue streams of rain illuminated by city lights. I always managed to get my assignments done wherever we were.

I glance at the clock. Another four hours until Jack would arrive. Finishing my paper, I grab a city map from the concierge and head south to the city. The weather was anything but accommodating for sightseeing. The roads, dotted with litter, had a kind of rusty color reminiscent of pollution. But given the time constraints, I wanted to make the most of it.

I park outside of Union Station and see the St. Louis arch peeking through a smokescreen of clouds and rain. The dilapidated buildings of downtown St. Louis hint to its industrial heyday, with faded advertisements of long ago, aged smokestacks and abandoned factories with punched out windows. Hopping over the rain puddles, I wander around Union Station. It was a quintessential tourist haunt, comprised of eateries, information kiosks and gift shops. I stop at a Hard Rock and pick up a magnet, adding to my growing souvenir collection.

* * *

"Hey you..." Sighing, Jack plops into the rental.

"Hi. How was your flight?"

"Lovely. Can't stand Atlanta airport. But I'm here. What'd you find out for dinner?"

"Well, I found—"

"Hold on, hold on I've got to get this. This is one of my guys."

"Hey Ned, yes let's go with that merger with United. And I don't care about what Shell says, I want it done and I want it done now. The quarterly report is due in two days. Got it?"

Yikes. He's noticeably agitated. I drive north, heading to the hotel. Scrolling down through my GPS, it had a library of previous destinations: the Fielmont in Dallas, the Intercontinental and Waldorf-Astoria in NYC, and now a Beechwood in Missouri was added to that growing gypsy list.

* * *

Twenty minutes later we exit the desolate stretch of highway and make our way toward The Hill, St. Louis' ethnic Italian neighborhood. Cozy bungalow houses amid tree-lined streets are lit by one forlorn orange streetlight. We park outside a tidy brick building with a small neon sign that reads Charlie's, Italian food.

With his hand outstretched on the table, my fingers are intertwined with Jack's. Those long, smooth fingers that I'd become long accustomed to caress mine with a tight embrace. Jack sucked at verbal expression and liked to deflect. One had to read his nonverbal cues, for that was what spoke volumes.

"I'm really happy you're here." His eyes cast a yellow hue with the flicker of candlelight. A meal of South African lobster tail and filet arrives and smiling, my eyes dart down at the table.

This was a habit of mine I hadn't quite outgrown

from the initial days of getting to know him, when the intimidation factor was still fresh and he had the ability to make me shiver from a prolonged stare. Subsequently, our years of spending many minutes, hours, and days together had rendered him a peculiar expert in reading my mannerisms.

"What are you nervous about?" He asks, pointing the fork at me.

"Nothing. I have no idea what you mean."

"I see that freckle moving."

I take my hair and cover up the freckles across my chest.

"It's moving. Drink some more wine it'll get better. You'd think by now you'd be used to this you nerd—but a hot one at that."

I chuckle.

"What else would you be doing right now if I hadn't come out?" I ask.

"Probably sitting in my room flicking between Sports Center and Law & Order."

"Well, I'm happy I'm here. Because I know you; I know that you would've came back to that lonely hotel room, laid your bags down, looked around at the imposing walls and said to yourself, there's something missing."

"Some Lara."

"Precisely. Babe, I...I came out because to think of you unhappy makes me incredibly unhappy. And although I know you're fully capable of taking care of just carrying on day to day on an unsatisfied note, I wanted to be here for you."

"Don't worry about me. I'm beyond help."

I clench his hand tight.

"But I do worry about you. Do you ever think about your happiness?"

"No, not really. But you help."

"See that's the danger of settling. You throw your hands up and say, well this is the best it's going to get, because I'm not changing and she's not changing. And so, you guys carry on day to day in a kind of obligatory rut, right?"

"Nailed it. Don't get married."

Next came a long silence, but I expected this much. I had always been the one who was more articulate when it came to expression. The poor guy sat there, transfixed in the slew of words that had just exited my mouth, trying to wrap his head around how spot-on I was.

"How does it get to that point?" I ask.

"What point?" Jack looks down; I can tell he's getting uncomfortable with the questions.

"I mean how does it get to the point where your going into strip clubs with backup T-shirts, carrying on with a second phone, and flying around other women with you while you collect frequent flyer miles?"

"I don't know…" He trails off. I look at him quizzically. He did know—he just didn't want to tell me. To see a man in a sense, numb to the point of no fucks given where he continuously shit all over his wife with no remorse had me reeling. But then, I could be her. I could be the wife who bought all the lies and slept next to a philanderer but still believed in the fortitude of those vows she'd taken long ago.

"Young and dumb, like I told you. My bachelor party was hilarious. Stacy Evans. Every guy wanted to bang her in college. Man, she had a great ass. My frat buddies got her to come by the night of my bachelor party. I fucked her brains out upstairs in my room. That chick was hot."

"Seriously?" I couldn't believe what I'd just heard.

"Yeah, had to get it out of my system. One last time, well… only it wasn't."

"And then you got married the following day?"

"Yep."

I get this vision of a blushing bride making her way down the altar, grinning ear to ear as she's presented to her husband. But then she's being given to a pig of a man—and all of his groomsmen too. Oh my god this poor woman. She'd married the wrong guy; a sociopath who couldn't keep it in his pants.

"Crème brûlée madam." The waiter arrives with two spoons and some port. I didn't want any, but like that ever mattered.

"Cheers. Thanks for coming." Jack winks as we toast glasses—and not a streak of decency for what he'd just discussed. I down the port.

"Babe. I am full, I—"

"I know."

36

Back at the hotel, we follow our well-rehearsed protocol over the years—walking in together with one of us always a few steps ahead. Passing meekly through the lobby, I head up to my room. My window was perfect for voyeurs—angling right down into the lobby. Crouching down beside my window I sit there in the darkness, watching him as he trots back to the elevators. Such a conflicted and beautiful, fucked up mess of a man.

"What are you doing?" He asks over the phone.

"Getting situated in my room. What are you doing?"

"Checking into my room. It's 517. What's yours?"

"507."

"Ha. Okay. See you soon."

I move down the hallway in my socks. This wasn't the Waldorf-Astoria.

"Hey you," closing the door quietly behind me.

"So, O'Fallon. A lot going on huh?" He lies there outstretched in his underwear, a *Wall Street Journal* outstretched over him.

"Ha. Hardly. Almost a close second to New York."

"So you went downtown St. Louis today?"

"Yeah. Despite the weather being shitty I still saw a few sights. The heartland of America wasn't all the bad. What time do you fly back tomorrow?"

"A few hours after you. I've got four meetings tomorrow and you've got class tomorrow. Get your assignment done?"

"Yes sir."

"Okay. I expect to see an A. It's a hard life you know, being in St. Louis for all of 36 hours and then jetting back to class the next day."

His sarcasm was tenfold.

"Yes someone's selfish tendencies don't leave much room for any choices. Just have to get it done." I quip, rolling my eyes.

Lying there in the sheets, his heavy frame leans in over mine as he takes one lonely index finger, tracing it along my hipbones, gliding it along my concave midriff. His forehead touches mine and I know what's coming next.

"Did you eat tonight? Damn, skinny."

Rolling my shirt over my head, the lights go off.

* * *

A sliver of blue light crept in from the window. I rub my eyes. Oh my god, my pelvis—what the hell did we do last night? Well at least there was no hair clumps this time. 6:00 AM. I roll over and see Jack in the bathroom, meticulously combing that hair.

"Miss you already. Have fun today, go see the arch." Slinging his backpack over one shoulder, he comes to the bedside and kisses me on the forehead, leaving $500 on the nightstand. There was a kind of vicarious nature that he lived through along my winding adventures from city to city. I suppose to hear about them served as some happy respite from his monotonous reality of conference calls and hiring and firings; the otherwise hum-drum society of corporate governance.

9:00 AM. I'd fallen back asleep for a few hours. I stand, slightly dizzy from the port last night and head to the bathroom. It stings to pee. *Oh my god, what the hell did he do to me last night?* I pat my parts and put a fresh pair of panties on. I had a limited time window on my last day in St. Louis—my plane would be taking off at 1:30. Stashing $100 for walk around, I hit the bank for a deposit and was off.

* * *

Burrowing my face in my scarf, I scurry down the small tree lined path leading to the arch. It was March but the wind still had an arctic nip to it—or maybe I was showing my Florida colors right now. Egg-like contraptions accommodating three people shakily carried you up the perimeter of the arch, definitely not for the claustrophobic. My egg was shared with two college age guys, one a redhead with a frizzy beard and a filthy backpack. The other a nerdy, mousy haired boy scribbling notes down onto a pad of paper. Our minutes spent together in the egg could go two directions: awkward or friendly, and so I broke the dry silence.

"So are you guys locals?"

Frizzy beard answered first.

"No, visiting my friend here," He points to his mousy haired cohort. "I'm from Kentucky. Never been to the arch. You?" I surmised frizzy beard's dental habits were the same as his filthy backpack, as his breath was something rancid. What a debacle to be in: in an egg with someone with halitosis to the second power.

"Oh I'm here for work. Done for the day so thought I'd go see the landmark of St. Louis." "Oh? What is it that you do?" The nerdy one chimed in.

"Charters Enterprises. We have a site here in O'Fallon."

All my traveling with Jack had made for a polished tagline, one free of hesitancy with an uncanny delivery.

The nerdy one's eyebrows shot up. "O'Fallon? That's close to where I'm from. Grown up in St. Louis all my life."

Our egg ride sputtered to a halt before any more questions could fill the air. I took a gulp of fresh air.

"Well, have a good trip guys. Nice meeting you both."

The view from the top was impressive, even on this overcast spring day; much of St. Louis was visible. I peered down to Union Station where I was last night.

"Do you feel that?" An elderly woman asks, a pair of binoculars hanging from her neck.

"Yeah," I look down at my feet. "What is that?"

An employee smiles at us, both looking like skittish tourists right about now.

"Oh that's just the arch. It sways in the wind."

"Oh. Well that's comforting." I say, wide eyed.

Are you fucking kidding me! Time for a drink.

* * *

It was closing in on 1:30. I round up my souvenirs: a bumper sticker, a postcard of the Arch, a brochure on Union Station and my magnet from the Hard Rock, stashing them in my carryon. Heading to my gate, I followed the domed ceiling corridors of Lambert airport, smiling at the clever design that mirrored that of the arch itself.

I slide up to a bar full of men armed with work laptops and button down shirts and order a glass of Cabernet. An assembly line of planes takes off one by one.

*You at the airport yet?

*Yes.

*Cool. I take off in three hours. Gotta finish this last meeting. Safe flight and good luck in class tonight.

37

The muggy clinch of the sunshine state greets me as I follow I-4 out of Orlando, taking it to 95 on the two-hour stretch north to Marsh Harbor. My books for tonight's class sit in the passenger seat. Jack was likely in the air right now, I thought about him and his dismal life. On all of our travels, I likened myself to something of a tour guide, showing him parts of Dallas, New York and now St. Louis that were beyond that familiar drab of the office. And then I thought about our dinner last night. What about her—I could be the wife, standing in the middle of some sprawling abode, packing lunches and going to soccer games, being blissfully deceived. Had she any idea of the sordid double life that her husband had kept? Communication between the two wasn't too high on the priority list. Jack had always kept his regular phone on the nightstand, and I had yet to hear it ring at least once on our excursions.

* * *

I sit in class trying to appear interested in the lecture. At two and a half hours, tonight seemed to drag on more than usual. Maybe that was due to some jet lag and a sharp tinge of pain that ping-ponged in my head. No wonder they served port in tiny glasses; apparently it didn't take much to give you a hangover.

"Miss Arbour, can you read aloud your summary for chapters three through six?"

Professor Dooley walks toward my desk. An awkward, short man whose neck kind of fused with his shoulders, he was always fidgeting with a pencil during lecture, always something between his fingers.

"Sure."

Shaking off my headache I sit upright and read aloud my summary, on point despite the nomadic pulse of my life.

* * *

"Ow!" Mosquito bites were the norm—or the "noseeums" as the southerners liked to call them—as you took the path that cut across the main lawn of campus to the parking deck. I preferred campus at night: the rat race of freshmen in pimped out Cavaliers and Honda Civics was absent, replaced by a mellow ambiance. I could have parked in the economy lot and taken a campus shuttle every time I went to class, but I paid the $95 per semester to park in the premium lot, or more aptly: the parking deck. It was only 9:00 P.M. but I was spent. At this hour, the parking deck is pretty deserted, my own footsteps echoing as I climb up to the second floor to my car.

"Oh hey Lara."

"Holy sh-shit Matt you scared the hell out of me!" I stammered.

Matt sat on the opposite side of the room in Professor Dooley's class. Lanky and with broad shoulders and the hint of some peach fuzz on his chin, he looked as if he wasn't completely done with growth spurts.

"Tired? I must have counted twenty yawns from you tonight."

"Wow, someone was paying attention. Yeah, you know, college life. Coffee is my best friend lately."

"Yeah I totally forgot to write up my summary for tonight. Dooley said I could turn it in next week for a ten point deduction."

"Oh yeah? Shoot ten points?"

I was pretty sure Matt was a stoner. The kid had missed maybe three classes already this semester and he definitely didn't travel like I did. His perpetually glazed over eyes and occasional musk of reefer were a dead giveaway. My phone begins to ring from inside my purse.

"Oh shoot. Sorry I've got to grab this. I'll see you next week!"

"Alright, see you Lara."

I wait for him to disappear down into the stairwell to answer Jack's call.

"Yo. How was class?"

"Was good, kind of boring. I was admittedly dragging tonight. In fact I just ran into one of my classmates who had counted my yawns tonight."

"Wow, maybe he's got a crush on you."

"Oh my god seriously? Kid's too young for me."

"I just left the airport a bit ago. Back to paradise and all over again tomorrow morning. Did you put that $500 in the bank today?"

"Yep, did it in St. Louis."

"Very good. Well, it was fun. I'll let you go be a nerd and do some homework."

"You know, some of us are trying to graduate sometime next year." I mutter.

"Hey, it's not easy being in Jack's world. It's fun, but it's not easy being in such high demand all the time."

"Ha, that it is. Good night babe."

38

I was happy at my new Marsh Harbor address but there was one problem. The fitness center here was less than mediocre; it downright sucked. A treadmill from maybe 1995 stood idly next to some free weights and no TV. One day going to get some groceries, I drove past an L.A. Fitness. I joined right away.

* * *

"And to your left is the sauna, and through these doors is the lap pool." I trail behind a guy named Wesley, a tanned and toned personal trainer giving me a tour. The gym was brand new, as they had only moved into the building two months ago. Rows of treadmills and ellipticals shine under fluorescent lights and weight training equipment stood surrounded by floor to ceiling mirrors. Three racquetball courts carried on intense games of men in sweatbands and goggles as slammed a ball around violently.

"Have you ever joined a gym before?" Wesley asks.

"No, this is my first." I say, fumbling with my water bottle.

"Well, I want you to know you've made a wise choice. We hold our members up high, and want to make sure you get a satisfactory workout each and every time you come in Miss Lara."

Miss Lara. My god, I was in the south. With Florida, it seemed the further north you got, the more southern everybody else was. Amazing feat of demographics it was.

"Ok thank you. I'm sure I'll be seeing you around. Thanks for the tour." Wesley promptly greets another customer waiting for a tour.

I head back to the locker room. CNN blared the latest on Obama's floundering budget plan. Women of all ages, stripped down to reveal saggy breasts, protruding stomachs and even unshaved nether regions. I began to wonder which was worse: the strip club locker room or the gym?

"My, my, my child you've got a fantastic stomach. How much abdominal work do you do?"

A husky black woman of about fifty with cornrows stood ogling me.

"Oh," I gush. "That's just a low- carb diet and some serious willpower." I refrain from sharing the six years or so of dancing under my belt that had contributed to my cut physique.

"Well God bless you, Lord!"

"Well thank you." I leave to explore the gym. Rows of brawny men exert themselves on weights and women ran into oblivion on the treadmills as I walked the aisles. I think I'll find myself here often.

* * *

I wipe cold beads of sweat from my neck. Three miles on the treadmill went by rather fast. Gathering my belongings, I check my phone. Three new messages and a missed call. Jack.

* Missed call?

* Too busy?

*Nerd

I scoff at the clock. It's only 5:00. He never get out this early.

*Oh pardon me while I took some time for fitness

Within minutes, a text.

*Sport bra?

*Yes

*Hot. But you're still in trouble.

*Whatever

39

Stowing my gym bag in the locker, I toss my phone in too, hoping I'd come back to find a call or text. I hadn't heard from Jack all day. This was unlike him. I stick M.I.A in my ears and push out nearly one hundred twenty crunches on the ab press. The gym was bustling with the after five-workday rush. Women gyrate in a choreographed Zumba class. Men and women alike sweat it out in Spin. Grunts are tenfold in the weight room.

I walk to the water fountain, passing by the racquetball courts. One court was electric; four men aggressively play, their sweat droplets littering the floor. I watch as they run, diving and colliding for a blue ball, smacking it violently against the wall. I knew nothing of the game but it looked a lot like tennis to me.

A pair of dark, slanted eyes glance at me from behind goggles. I silently mouth *hi* and take off bashfully.

* * *

6:00 already. Where had the time gone? Passing by the racquetball courts to exit, I saw him again. He was cute, with a red bandana splayed across his forehead that wicked away sweat. Considerably shorter than Jack, he stood at a humble 5'7" or so. His black hair was cut in a crew cut, very close to his head. I presumed a possible military background. And then a thud. Good job. My phone lay there, bruised but hopefully not broken. I crouch down to pick up the damned thing and then a pleasant, disarming voice.

"Hello there."

Peering up, it was him.

"Hi," I say shakily. "Can I help you with that?"

"Oh no, no, I've got it. Just slipped out of my bag somehow I guess."

"Yeah, I'm surprised my iPhone even still works given how many times I've dropped it."

Smiling, I retrieved my bruised piece of technological machinery, hoping the blood would leave my face soon.

"I'm Dave." He said, extending his hand. Those dark slants slightly crinkled at the edges.

"Lara."

"So I've never seen you here before. Are you new?"

"No, not entirely. I moved to Marsh Harbor in September for the Coastal College of Florida."

People I didn't know well only got the very the tip of the iceberg, omitting the root of the motivation in me moving here: to be closer to the man who had become such a driving force in my life, a daily, infiltrating magnitude of desire and control so intoxicating I knew not how to escape it. But I wasn't sure I *wanted* to either.

"Ah. What are you studying?"

Sweating profusely, he removed his bandana; tributaries of sweat running along his skin.

"It's a bachelors of English."

"So you like to write. Have you ever played racquetball?"

"No but it looks fun. It's gotta be one hell of a cardio

workout."

"Totally. Tell you what, come here tomorrow around five and I'll show you the ropes."

40

June 2013

"How's school going?" Dave asks as I enter the court. He had on a pink bandana today, with one hand covered in a racquetball glove.

"It's going good, roughly a year and a half left and I'll be done—coffee willing. I'm taking summer classes so I get done faster. What does that do?" I point to the glove.

"Gives you more grip on the racquet."

"I will have to invest in one of those seeing as I'll be playing more often."

"Yes, and to no ones disappoint might I add." Dave's eyes light up.

"So. This is how you throw a serve." Motioning himself behind me, he gently grasps my hips with one hand while the other is on my racquet, simulates a swing motion.

"You let the ball drop from your hand, and then with a strong backswing, whack it. The goal is to hit the wall with one bounce, not two after it descends from the wall. This is how you make a point."

Trying to concentrate on this racquetball lesson was proving to be difficult. I liked him. I actually liked another guy. "So what do you do?" I ask.

"I'm a pilot."

"Oh really? Private or commercial?"

"Commercial. JetBlue. I go to the islands a lot. Puerto Rico. St. Croix. Dominican. Not a bad view from the office."

Hitting the ball back and forth, we're joined by Tim and Rafael, a Hispanic silver- haired player, sporting a synchronized shirt and shoes in neon yellow. Tim looked like the all American dad, with white Reeboks and white tube socks to match. A wiry mullet crept down the back of his neck.

"Ah so we found where Dave was hiding." Tim called as I hit the first serve.

"Trying to help the girl amp her game up!" Dave answered, swerving about the court, trying to block Tim's strong swing.

"Wow you're pretty. No wonder Dave wants to play with you. Dave has never once offered to amp up any of our games." Tim said plaintively, his eyes peering down to the waxed court floor. I let out a chuckle.

Rafael slams the ball and scores a point, refocusing us into the game.

I wipe one lonely bead of sweat from my brow.

"Say, I'm famished. You hungry?"

"Yeah, I usually cook but I could go for something light. You got any ideas?"

"Yeah I do. Meet me out in the parking lot."

* * *

 Walking out, I see Dave sitting idly in his car, tucked under an oak tree in a back corner of the gym lot.

"Won't you come in?" He called.

I imagined my mom screaming at me right now for this

stunt, but I proceeded anyway.

"Hello there," An amiable childlike grin overtook his face. Gone were those aggressive mugs I'd seen on the racquetball court all these weeks.

"Hi, what's going on?" My hands fall reticently in my lap, legs tightly coiled atop each other. This leather interior is singing my skin.

"So, I have to say. To have you here in my car right now, is quite an honor."

Jolt. Oh wow. What the hell do I say to that? I decided to downplay like Jack always did with me. It didn't work.

"Oh stop, I am nothing."

"Oh no, you're definitely something; I can assure you. That day you came in and walked past the courts, you damn near stopped the game. Did you know that?"

"No, I must have missed that memo."

"Everybody was just kind of like, *who* is that?"

"Really?" The cynicism was palpable in my voice.

"Yes, really. Girls like you don't come into the gym often. Have you looked around?"

Smirking, I peer down to nowhere in particular.

"Ah yeah, I guess you've got a point."

"I think there's only you and maybe two other girls who have amazing bodies in there. The rest—well, let's just say they're are all dying to look like you."

"Well hey you've got to start somewhere right?"

"Yep. So what do you do in your free time?"

I knew this one was coming. I start beating myself up mentally. Why had I given him my number? Why was I sitting in this very car? Why was I over thinking this? It was just a conversation. It would be just a bite to eat. Right?

"I uh, I am very busy with school. I'm taking three classes at CCF."

"So what do you do when you're not in school?"

"I usually hang with my good friend Sarah or workout. Or travel. Here's Sarah."

Dave's eyebrows shoot up as I show him a shot of Sarah and I from a night out in Marsh Coral Cove back in November.

"Wow, you two are sure to break some hearts together.

So what else? Do you travel?"

"Oh yeah, I love to travel. Spontaneous trips are the best."

"Where have you been?"

"Well, as far as international goes, Norway and Switzerland. And domestic, Dallas, New York City and St. Louis to name a few."

"Well, you're quite a well traveled young lady."

"I am? Two foreign countries?"

"That's more than most Americans."

"True." Nodding my head in agreement, I turned the questions on him before he could get another one out.

"So how long have you been a pilot?"

"About ten years now. I started out in the navy. Moved around a lot due to that, but Marsh Harbor is my final resting place."

"Nice."

I looked to the time on his dash. 6:15. Not that he had a usual time in recent months past, but Jack usually got out anywhere between 6:00 and 7:30.

"So where do you want to eat?"

"Um, well, actually I think maybe a smoothie could suffice. I'm sorry, not that hungry all of a sudden. My appetite's quite dysfunctional."

"Oh. Okay, well, how about we go to the Smoothie Shack off San Jose?"

"Ok, let me lock my car." Pulling away, I look at my car as my nerves shot my appetite. What was I doing wrong? Grabbing a smoothie—with another guy.

* * *

I slurp through a big red straw, looking wide eyed at Dave. I found my mind drifting to the frantic finance world of Jack and Charters Enterprises and expensive dinners and hotel rooms—something I had become familiar with over the past few years, but none of it could be found here. This was something new, something fresh.

"So what are you doing the rest of the day?" Dave asked.

"Just some errands and domestic things I suppose."

I was trying to sound as uninteresting as possible, but I feared that it was too late for that.

"Well, you should probably be going then. You know,

did I ever mention that I get these perks as a pilot? They're called buddy passes. Ever heard of them?"

I damn well knew what buddy passes were but played dumb.

"No, what exactly are those?"

"Well, I get so many a year, and, to date the only person I've given some to are my chiropractor. I figured since you've already been to Europe a few times, maybe you'd be interested in joining me on some travels elsewhere. Like Costa Rica or Hawaii."

Oh my god. This guy was inviting me to a front row seat of free travel. I hid my nerves behind my forced smile. I didn't want to hurt the guy. He was innocent and starry eyed. He liked me a lot that much was obvious. But it wasn't right to drag him into my debacle of a love life.

"Are you bribing me?"

"Possibly."

"Well, I will think on it. Talk later?"

"Sure, looking forward to it."

"Thanks for the smoothie."

41

Home. I hurriedly shut the door behind me and sink into myself. A kind of dizziness overtakes me and I let out a sigh of relief. 7:00 P.M and Jack hadn't called yet. I couldn't move two inches into my apartment, frozen against the door. Pulling my knees to my chest, my breaths echo within my ears. Small tears began to well up in my eyes.

For the first time in my life with Jack, I feel trapped. Trapped between my personal happiness and financial security. Money had never equated to happiness to me, it only enabled you to live a comfortable life, affording security and freedom. But who really wanted to struggle? While the other kids in my classes were stressing about tuition funds, I already knew where mine was coming from.

For the first time, I took a good, hard look at my own happiness, and questioned it. Was it my own or just some dream that was bought?

* * *

Was I happy? Hadn't I been anything but happy for these past few years? Yes. Jack was the first man that I had truly fallen for. A strong, perpetual love that had transcended the course of damn near three years. A love that had intimidated while inspiring me. Indeed, I was lucky. I had financial stability, a fleet of frequent flyer miles and had seen destinations that topped the bucket lists of many. But for the first time, I felt what I never wanted to feel: which was more. I wanted more. More time. More love. I wanted more of more. I wanted to feel what *more* felt like.

From the beginning, I had told myself: it was not for me to want. It was not for me to feel. This entire thing was doomed from the beginning. I frantically reached inside my brain for that pragmatic reminder, begging for it to make an encore and come smack me in the face.

* * *

"So what are you doing tonight?" Dave asks. It was a Monday and the gym was booming. We were in the court again, working on my backswing.

"Oh, nothing interesting. Just a lot of reading for school."

"You wanna uh...you wanna go outside and talk more? I feel like the guys are spying on us."

"I think they may be jealous." I wink.

"I think you may be right."

We nonchalantly slip out, leaving Tim and the others lost in the game.

The sun was dipping below the horizon, and the smoldering blue of night began to emerge.

I found myself in that leather interior once again.

"So what did you say you're doing tonight?" Dave asked, zeroing in close to my face. I peered at the time. 7:15. I hadn't heard from Jack all day. A kind of tiny damsel in distress voice emerged from within me, secretly reaching out for Jack to come whisk me away.

But wasn't this what I wanted, to talk to Dave? To get to know him better? I remembered the reason from earlier today.

"I'm just gonna go home and cook some dinner for myself. Nothing exciting."

True I was purposely sounding less interesting than I really was. Because I could feel the next question coming and that would get shot down with flying colors. Because he wasn't Jack. Because I had not had any other man for all these years. Because I was comfortable in my seclusion. Because I wanted to tell myself I didn't need more.

With Dave's hand on my thigh, a fused shudder of fear and exhilaration sweeps over me. I think of Jack; he had never done that, not this soon. In fact, a good few months had passed before he even remotely did something like that. Pulling me close so that I was stretched across the center console, Dave nuzzles my cheek with his lips, delivering minute pecks.

"You are beautiful, you know that?"

I sit there in the passenger seat like some robotic mannequin, giving obligatory affection. You want to hug me? I'll hug you back. My nerves rendered me useless, without a compass of what to say or do. The creeping fear that Jack would be calling anytime had me on edge.

"Well I'm pretty hungry, and got a good deal of reading to do tonight. It was nice seeing you. Always a fun time at the gym."

"Likewise. Nice seeing you Lara."

Giving an obligatory nod, I smiled and was out. A long droned out sigh exits my lips as I head home. And then a ring; it wasn't Jack.

"You know, I'm kind of hungry too. Got no food at home."

"You are?" I said amicably.

A flood of thoughts entered my head. What else would I be doing tonight? Sitting at home, doing homework, staring at the wall and relishing in my solitude, like every night. Dave was really the first man I had let in outside of my clandestine world with Jack. And what was Jack likely doing right now? Probably at home eating a fast food dinner, kissing his wife with a deceitful mouth and acting remotely interested in this weekend's impending sport schedule for the kids.

"What do you usually do for dinner?" I ask him as I made my way up the stairs to my door.

"Well, I don't really eat that well. That's part of the reason I'm at the gym so often. A pilot's schedule doesn't really allow for healthy eating between layovers."

Pulling out a skillet, I drizzled a chicken breast some Sherry wine.

"What do you like to cook?"

"Well being that I'm Sicilian, I was raised among good cooks. We never had any of that Chef Boyardee, Ragu or Prego stuff."

"So you guys had the homemade stuff."

"Precisely."

Why did I have to like Dave? I had not even as much as looked as another guy in these past two years with Jack and now suddenly here I was, having an innocuous conversation with a guy from the gym about culinary delights. How did this happen? For the first time in two years with him, I had a refreshed perspective. I had no bounds. Jack liked to think I was bound to him, but this was the beauty of the situation; I wasn't.

Perhaps I was tired of everything being his way, all the time. I was tired of this kind of double standard. I was tired of lying down and donning a façade of passivity.

I didn't look at Jack and his dirty deeds and equate those to speak for all men. Jack, despite his immense place in my life and gratuitous, selfish nature, was a complex character. I had told myself this very thing—whatever it was—was what was right for us. I could never deal with someone like that full time. I never had a hankering for him to leave, but his increased possessiveness was becoming heavy.

* * *

"Lara? You there?" Dave shot me back into the conversation.

"Well why—why don't you just uh, come up then?" I stammered, holding the phone to my ear skittishly.

"Okay, let me turn around. Which building are you in?"

"I'm in building—"

Incoming call on the other line. It was Jack. *Oh my god!* I let it go to voicemail.

"Building twelve. Apartment twelve-twenty. Third floor. My mom is calling on other line can I get this please? I'm sorry."

"Sure, sure. See you soon."

Without fail, a text.

* No answer???

Holy shit. Dave would be here any minute. Jack hated to be refused. I dialed.

"Hey babe," I greet Jack in my usual coy banter.

"Missing my calls? What are you doing, you nerd?"

"Just cooking some dinner. You know, the healthy stuff you know and hate."

"Yeah, you're probably cooking some nerd concoction like, squash pasta or something."

"No babe, that was the other night."

Knock, knock.

Oh shit. The door. And I'm on the phone with Jack.

"Uh, hey babe, someone's knocking at my door. I think it's one of the neighbors from across the hall. Can I call you back?"

"Knocking on your door? Yeah, yeah. Later."

Pensively setting my phone down on the kitchen counter, my pulse echos in my ears. Letting out a sigh, I open the door.

42

Dave's eyes were big as golf balls as he removes his shoes.

"You've got yourself a nice little place here."

"Now *those* are some curtains," He smiled, moving toward the crackling stovetop.

"Whatcha makin'?" His dark slants for eyes had a cheerful gleam in them, I could tell how happy he was to be here. I still couldn't believe I actually told him where I lived.

"Oh just some chicken breasts in sherry and vegetables. The usual healthy choice for me."

"So this must be how you get that washboard stomach

I've seen at the gym."

Blushing, I shake my head as Dave slides one arm around my waist. I jerk.

"Wow, jumpy tonight?"

"Oh, ha," I try unsuccessfully to mask my bashfulness.

"Just surprised me was all. That's a little more contact than the usual racquetball game."

Pressing himself into me, I feel the faint rise of his erection. *Oh god. What the hell was I doing? Oh, but I liked him. A little bit. And he was single*. I cut into the chicken. Done. I set the table and we sit across from each other. The first time two people sat in here together and it wasn't even the guy who paid for the place. I pang of guilt hits me in the stomach. Had I lost my mind? I had. Suddenly I felt transparent. What if Jack called? I wanted Dave to leave, and soon.

"Looks good." Dave says, cutting into a chicken breast. I wondered if he picked up on my nerves, which were on haywire. I envied Jack's ability to remain effortlessly impassive, his stoic exterior all the more challenging to read. All these years and still, I was at a complete loss to what the man repressed deep within him.

"So really you could walk to the gym if you had to, huh? I didn't realize how close you were to it."

"Yeah, it's nice, definitely convenient. You and the rest of the racquetball guys are really the first group of people I've clicked with since moving up here aside from acquaintances at CCF. But other than that, I am very much on my own up here." I glance at my phone. Jack hadn't texted or called back. He must have been in for the night. Locked down. In this instance, it was actually a good thing.

"Living on your own can get lonely sometimes."

"Can it?" I seemed to be asking a question to which I already had the answer to, having floated between my prized solitude and newfound loneliness; something I never thought I'd experience. "I've always liked having my own space."

"Oh come on, a pretty girl like you surely wants someone to curl up with every once in awhile."

"Perhaps. But it's always nice to come home to an empty house and just expand in your solitude. There's nothing more freeing."

"True, but you don't always want it to be this way do you?"

"Not sure. Time will tell, won't it?" "Sure it will. Well, hey thanks for the great dinner. No wonder you look like you do. You eat well." Showing him to the door, Dave wraps his arms around me. *Oh god, what was happening?*

"Glad you enjoyed it."

"More than you know."

"I still can't believe you're here." I fail miserably to hold back my anxiety and let out a snort as I hang my head low.

"Well I can. It's nice to see you somewhere other than the gym." Whipping me around, Dave suddenly presses me against the door, diving into my mouth. I close my eyes. *Oh no. No, this is so wrong. I can't do this.* But this time I kiss him back, and it's not obligatory. Jack invades my conscience during those entirely too long seconds between.

"Thanks Lara. I'll be at the gym next Tuesday. Flying to San Juan this weekend. You wanna come?"

"Yep. I'll be right there." I jest, smiling at him.

"See you in a few days. I wanna practice on my backswing some more."

Closing the door behind him, I sink into a heaping pile of emotions.

What had I done? For the first time in my and Jack's existence, I had put first the very thing that I'd neglected so long: myself. That was, thinking about myself. This entire world with Jack was guarded and clandestine. I didn't let other people in toward myself. I didn't want anyone else in. I just wanted Jack. Or so I had thought. What was I doing? Following my instincts.

My time with Jack had made me ponder many things about life. The authenticity of relationships. The fortitude of someone's word. The resilience of love. What it can withstand. How it can be toppled. How it can be saved. Those who care about their relationships, and those who could give a shit.

There was always a motivating force behind these types of things. People don't act out for arbitrary reasons; usually there stands a palpable void somewhere in the person's life. Well if there was a void in mine, I had just become acquainted with it. And how long had it been there? Perhaps it was shrouded in denial, much like Jack's marriage, refusing to acknowledge the very big issues painted in red there. For the first time in my life, I found myself conflicted.

43

"Men compartmentalize, my dear." Sarah said on the other end of the phone. It was 8:30 in the morning, entirely too early but I had papers among papers to finish today. Finals beckoned. Summer A semester was done. This would be my last summer at CCF.

"Jack is a man of power. He's used to people doing things for him, when he asks of them. He's got the wife at home to take care of the kids, and he's got his hot little mistress on the side to take on trips and have fun with. Sorry for the terminology."

I was unmoved by her use of the term. All these years, I hadn't known exactly how to define myself. But I also had never been in a situation quite like this before either.

"What makes your situation different from the prototypical mistress tale is, he's taking care of you.

Very good care of you. He's putting you on a sort of pedestal, to be at his beckon call. You're kind of like a modern day kept woman dude!"

"Oh my god. I am."

"Well that's not entirely a bad thing."

"No, no not at all. Could be worse."

"I mean, the man's got the means."

"Yeah. I'm still dumbfounded by all of it. I still, on occasion, have a hard time accepting money from him. But, I've learned it doesn't make a bit of difference. He's going to do what he wants to do. He always has. And it is that same ideology that makes me thankful I am *not* married to him. I'm sure it's no walk in the park."

"Yeah, if his domineering behavior with you is any hint..."

I fight the urge to Google the term as I stare perplexed before my computer. I type in 'kept woman' and scroll through the definitions.

Kept Woman: Historically, the term has denoted a "kept woman", who was maintained in a comfortable (or even lavish) lifestyle by a wealthy man so that she will be available for his sexual pleasure. Such a woman could move between the roles of a mistress and a courtesan depending on her situation and environment. As the term implies, he was responsible for her debts and provided for her in much the same way as he did his wife, although not legally bound to do so.

Holy fuck.

44

"So two classes for six weeks? Not bad."

I throw the washcloth in the hamper with Jack's liquid on it. Being taken from behind was one way to be awakened in the morning. 6:30 A.M and he stands in my bathroom, face half-covered in shaving cream. His gym clothes sit in a pile on the floor, something that had now become a laughable plot escape. Lying there in the tangle of my sheets, I stare at him but see the silhouette of Dave instead and that bandana. I quietly smirk at the thought of him being in here all too recently, wondering if Jack could sense another man being on "his" territory.

I crawl out of bed and meet him in the bathroom, hugging him from behind. I close my eyes and I recall the initial days of our courtship: the envelopes, the incessant calls, the impromptu travel dates. It had all become so commonplace the last few years I thought nothing more of it until Dave came along.

That familiar pair of starched slacks with a perfect crease down the middle hangs from my dresser next to a dress shirt with the dry cleaner's tag still on it. The scent of Old Spice illuminates my apartment with sandalwood. It was like Jack lived here. But he didn't, I reminded myself.

"Okay, here's $400. I want you to go to the bank today, make a payment on the Discover, leave $100 out for walk around. Got it?"

"Got it." His businesslike tenor had over the years predisposed me to delivering a most prescribed response.

I look at my balances, texting him all of it. My vacation savings had a little over $1,500 in it. Roughly four weeks until summer B semester would start. My mind began to turn with possible "solocation" options.

* * *

Class drags on. I've become so distracted over the last few weeks. I look around to my classmates. My life isn't in the same category with theirs, living in dorms and throwing themselves into mountains of student loan debt. Were my issues as dire as theirs? No, but mine were on a vastly different scale. I wonder how that would go if I actually told one of them of my debacle: *Well you see, I've got this very married very domineering, overzealous mess of a man with more money than what he knows what to do with. And then there's this other guy who I like, but I feel guilty for liking.* Just then, Jack texts.

*You in class?

* Yes

*Come meet me in the parking lot of the Fresh Market. Got some cash for you.

Really? I can't. We're going over thesis options for midterms.

*Really? Some notice would be nice. I don't know, we're going over midterm stuff.

I wondered why he was over by the university as it was on the other side of Marsh Harbor. I sit there, blinking at my phone. Well I had never skipped out of class early.

Professor Levrett looks at me. She was a nazi about phones. Well, there was only forty-five minutes left anyway. I skip across the deserted campus lawn to the parking deck.

* * *

We sit in the empty parking lot of the Fresh Market. CCF was only two miles up but still, was the principal: it didn't matter what I had going on. It mattered that it was convenient for *him*. Like always.

"Really? Next time tell me. I can't just be skipping out of class like this at a moment's notice."

Flashing me a sardonic grin, he throws a butterfly clipped $1,200 in my lap.

"Sure you can. We did it all the time when I was in college." "Yeah well, that was, early nineties? The cool kids can't get away with everything those cool kids did in the nineties. Some professors deduct points for leaving early and absences."

"Perhaps, perhaps. Listen, I was over by CCF and thought I'd meet up and give you some cash. Take this for rent and car and put the rest in savings."

I look at him obligingly. For the first time, I look at him not with attraction but more so disdain. Is this how he got women to pay attention to him? To throw money at them for their time? All for what? To get off? To control? He didn't care about me or my schedule. It was always when it suited him.

"Okay, thanks babe."

Cupping my face, he gives me a deep kiss.I head home, class was over now. I thought back to my classmates. I could be them, struggling. I could be racking up thousands in debt. I could be, I could be…but I'm not.

45

"I'm going to Seattle." I tell Sarah on the other end of the phone.

"What? Why?"

"I don't know. I don't know. I just need some time to myself. In light of everything lately in my life, not that my life is completely fucked up—or maybe it is. I don't know. I've got the time, I've got the money. I need some time to decompress."

"I understand babe. When do you go?"

"June 17th through the 20th. And guess what airline? JetBlue."

"Haha, does Dave go there?"

"I don't know."

* * *

"So Seattle? Only nerds go there." Jack prods at me on his drive home from work.

"Yeah, I've got the time. Got some saved in the account. I want to go somewhere where I haven't been before summer starts."

"Yeah go. Maybe I can meet you before, give you some cash."

"Okay, yeah."

"When do you leave?"

"A week and a half."

"Cool. Alright, well maybe next Monday, we'll see how my schedule frees up."

Wow. A trip without him and he was offering to give me some spending money. Alright then.

* * *

The weekend had been lackluster. For the first time in my life, I could feel my heart being peeled from Jack. Saturday night had found me curled up in the fetal position, afraid and nervous but also very much in tune with what I was feeling, and more importantly what had brought me to this point. I did not have my own life. My life was very much centered on a selfish, conflicted mess of a man. I recalled how I felt that first time Dave walked into my apartment. Freaked out and huddled at the base of my door, in disbelief of what I had just done. But what *had* I done? Invited another guy of whom I was interested in to my home. But was it really my home? It was my home *kept* for Jack and I. I had denied myself my own happiness. I had denied myself freedom. I had denied myself true love. All for what? To be kept under a controlled world where the bait was financial security? I wanted a life to call my own.

46

"Flight 1242 to Seattle, we will begin the boarding process now."

I stood in the American Airlines terminal at Marsh Harbor airport. Only this time I was alone. Jack had never shown up for vacation funds. Whatever. I knew it was because I was taking a trip without him, one that didn't benefit him. Whatever. I had barely slept the past few nights, my mind racing with this newly minted crossroads in my life, torn between my own happiness and my happiness at the expense of someone else.

* * *

June in Seattle. I liked the way the Pacific Northwest did summer—no humidity. Some surmised the suicide rate dissipated during the summer, as residents were awakened from a kind of melancholy slumber brought on by the brooding clouds here. My first day here was a beautiful one. The sun had come out of its elusive shell. Pike Place was alive with locals and tourists alike savoring freshly sliced fruit. A crowd of Asian tourists armed with cameras stood outside the original Starbucks, sipping coffee. Art vendors were busy with potential buyers perusing their talents. Sunbathers and homeless alike congregated on the lawn at Victor Steinbrueck Park, nonchalantly passing marijuana among each other—after all it was legal here.

I checked my phone. Nothing from Jack. He hadn't given me any money for this trip. I felt it to be a kind of subliminal dig of resentment as I was taking a trip without him. Regardless, I wanted to be alone. The next two days would be a much-needed respite. Boats cruised the Puget Sound with squalls of tourists snapping photos. The space needle was alive with selfie takers. Pike Place Market merchants and their sales tactics lured you to come in and take a look at their goods. Picking up two pieces of art from a local artist, I bought a ticket for the Argosy waterfront cruise and hopped in, eager to see Seattle from the water. I was the only one solo on the cruise, but I didn't care. To feel the crisp summer breeze and get lost in the ambiance of Seattle's distinct skyline was more than enough for me.

47

7:00 P.M. Today had been epic. I had climbed to the top of the Space Needle, toured the Chihuly Garden of glass and marveled at Pioneer Square, and taken in the minty aroma of the infamous Gum Wall. My hotel, a Comfort Inn, was far from the opulent stays I've had with Jack in New York and Dallas. But that's not why I came to Seattle. Tossing my bag of art on the bed, I check my phone. Nothing. This was a first. Jack was always up my ass. *He's mad I am on a trip outside of his control. Unreal.* Whatever.

I climb into the shower. It's cold and porcelain. Strangely, I feel at ease in this unfamiliar room. But hadn't it always been this way? If anything I had fine-tuned my adaptive nature over the years. I fashion myself on the bottom, letting the water hit my knees. Only it's not warm—it's lukewarm. *What the fuck.* And then tears—out of nowhere. I didn't know what was happening. I wanted so desperately to hold on to the clandestine world Jack and I had created over the years, but I felt my cares shifting from his needs to my own. For years, my very life had been constructed to appease his. My class schedule, my time, my living quarters—all too pacify a man who got off on control. And what did I get? Someone who was borrowed. But hadn't I been okay with that? I mean, I could be her—kissed with the deceitful mouth, shit on night every night as her husband rammed some other chick on yet another business trip, as she sat blissfully unaware in her Stepford Wife community.

I wrap myself in a towel and collapse on my bed. I can't remember a time where I gave a moment to myself during any of this. My priority was always him. Always striving to make him happy, to take his pain, to relax him, to simply be in his company in a kind of foggy servitude that was losing its rose colored cloak.

* * *

"Ah, Florida! That's where we're from. Fort Lauderdale to be exact. Wherabouts?"

An older couple sits a table ahead of me in the dining room of the hotel as I eat my breakfast. I place them in their late fifties. Today was my last day in Seattle.

"Oh yeah. I live in Marsh Harbor. I don't really consider

it to be the quintessential Florida. That's south for sure!"

"We're here celebrating our thirtieth wedding anniversary. From here we're heading to Victoria, British Columbia to see the whales. You should really try and get up there if you've got a chance. Stunning."

"Oh yeah, I've never been up to British Columbia but it sure looks amazing."

"You know a place you should check out by night is Queen Anne hill. It's some high dollar real estate in Seattle but has the best view of the city. And on a clear day, you might be able to see Mt. Rainier. So are you here with a boyfriend, or?" asks the husband. Older people always got a hall pass on being intrusive. They were just trying to make conversation.

"No, I'm here alone. I wanted to see Seattle, I've never been. So I came."

The wife's eyebrows shot up.

"Wow, I really envy the bravery you have. By your age, I already had three kids and had never seen much outside of my hometown. See the world while you can."

"Well thanks you guys, I'll see what I get into today. Back to the sunshine state tomorrow."

48

I stand idly on the overlook that is Queen Anne hill. I'd followed that kind old man's advice and was I ever grateful I did. The view was spectacular. The space needle was illuminated in a pearlescent yellow that reflected off into the night sky, and a kind of plum haze from the city's glow hung like a canopy above.

I wasn't alone here. Groups of boisterous high schoolers in formalwear—perhaps it was prom season— stood nearby, snapping photos with the space needle in the background. Photographers were perched on the edge with tripods, all vying for the perfect night shot of Seattle. Queen Anne, despite being a residential area, was a landmark abuzz with tourists and locals alike all trying to capture the beautiful skyline. It was summer but it was cool and brisk, I loved it. Not a drop of mugginess in the air. I moved to the edge and snapped a few photos. I thought to Jack and how I wished he could be here to see this. But then I reminded myself: I was living for me now. Not for him.

Today had not been as jam-packed as yesterday but my trip to Seattle was a successful one. Gone from my mind was the distinct heaviness of control back home; also gone was this newfound struggle I found myself in, things had become clearer. A stark realization of what I wanted shook me out of this stupor that I had been living in for too long. I stopped looking at Jack for what I wanted to him to be, but for what he really was.

49

July 2013

I frame a photograph of myself at Queen Anne, looking at it pensively. Only three days had seemed like a lifetime. I felt refreshed. I never knew what neglect really meant until recently. I hadn't from Jack while in Seattle, and the three days there without a peep from him was telling. A trip without him? No money. A trip with him? Money. I was so over the double standards. But I wasn't livid pissed about it. Summer B had begun. My final year at CCF.

* * *

Lacing up my shoes, I pack my racquets in the bag and head for the door, until a knock has me frozen in my steps. Was it Jack? He was never out before five. It was probably some Baptist inviting me to their church with a live band. I peer through the peephole. *Oh my god.*

* * *

"You're late. You said you'd be at the gym two hours ago." It was Dave, standing there in that bandana. He looked delicious; tiny drips of sweat forming a small trail around his feet.

"I thought you said 4:00?"

"No, I said 2:00. I played a few games of racquetball, did weights, some cardio. Thought, okay she should be here soon. Then did some more cardio, you still weren't there."

"Awe, I'm sorry still putting stuff away from my trip. "

I stood there in the doorway, frantically searching my brain for something more to say.

"Well you gonna just stand there or let me in?"

"Oh yeah, yeah, sure come in. Would you like a water?"

He sits Indian-style on the floor, a dank odor emanating from him. But I didn't care. I was happy to see him, albeit unexpectedly.

"So do you always do unannounced visits?" I sit beside him, reclining on my arms.

He lets out a chuckle, gulping some water

"No. Is it okay?"

"Sure, yeah." I say nervously. I look at the door—the same door he had pressed me up against a while back. That was hot.

"Ugh! Thanks!" Giving me a playful shove, I was now just as sweat-ridden as him.

"Oh, look at that, guess you've gotta take a shower with me now."

"Well, an A for effort."

I wipe the newly placed oil slick off my shoulder and Dave leaps atop me, pressing himself between my legs. Two drops of sweat fall on my chest.

"Oh god, alright, alright!"

Dragging me to my feet, he scoops me up over his shoulder and carries me to the bathroom.

"Was this premeditated?"

"No, just wanted to take a shower."

Right. Watching him in disbelief, the undresses in my bathroom as if he lived here. My mouth drops open at the sight of his hardware. I thought only tall guys had bigger ones—apparently not.

"Well, what are you waiting for? You've gotta get that sweat off, don't you?"

Oh my god, what was I doing? In the shower, with another man? I didn't hear much else except for the patter of water. I didn't feel much else except the yearning behind Dave's hands. They touched me differently than Jack, his curious hands cupping my breasts softly. Standing there under the water, tiny waves of trepidation were toppled by enjoyment, a manifestation of something I could have at my own beckoned call.

"You feel so nice," he whispers as he nips at my ear.

He was behind me now, his erect penis poking my lower back. A branching feeling crept within me. I looked into those dark eyes. Instead of cold and mercurial, I saw hope, happiness, and adoration. I wanted to take his hand and get lost with him. Or perhaps I wanted to be found.

"Turn this way,"

With his hands on my hips, he rhythmically moves his penis in and out between my soapy legs. *I am not having sex with him. I am not having sex with him.* I don't even know what to do, what to think at this moment. Perhaps that was my problem: I thought too much.

"Haha, you're a dork."

"Hey, can you blame me? I mean look at you."

"Glad I'm not a guy. Sounds difficult. I'm getting out."

A few moments later out comes Dave. I watch him speculatively from my bed, relishing the sight of another man here. Sure he stood at all of about 5'7" but was he ever so beautiful.

"Well, I think I've got all the sweat off. You?"

He dips over me, nuzzling my neck.

"Haha, yes, I think so. So we can no longer say only in your wet dream about that shower, huh?"

"Nope."

Throwing on a fresh Under Armour shirt over his head, I look plaintively at the sight of those shoulders going under. My, they were beautiful. And they were a far cry from Jack's freckled ones.

"You be at the gym later this week?"

"Yes, tomorrow. You?"

"Flying to San Juan. Wanna come?" His moxie was relentless.

"I can't," I roll my eyes, torn between the freedom that Dave represented and my kept life. But why couldn't I have both? Was I able to do both? Oh my god, what if Jack had been here? What if he'd knocked on that door during the shower? How would I have navigated that shit storm?

"Maybe sometime in the very near future." I say auspiciously.

"Well, happy I got my shower. See you next week."

* * *

"You didn't have sex with him? What!" Sarah shouts through the phone.

"My life has become *Sex and the City* Marsh Harbor

version, I swear."

"No it's not dude. You're just finally seeing the light after all these years. "

"Why did it take me this long to realize?"

"Simple. You're a woman. Your emotions get in the way. You know, there is some truth to that rose colored glasses analogy."

"Yeah, you're not lying. I mean Jack has given me a lot in life, things that I never asked for. But it's all been at a price. I mean, I never thought he would leave. I was always pragmatic about it. I'm not lonely but lately have begun to feel, well, isolated. What is my life? I go to school, I go to the gym. And now, I don't even work."

"Compartmentalize. Just like he has. You have a use for him, right?" Sarah had a point.

"Yes."

"Okay, so *you* make use of him. Set your heart aside and play the game."

"But what do I do if he calls and I'm out with Dave?"

"Don't answer. You don't have to."

"Yeah but that's easier said than done. Remember how

Jack had angrily texted me that night Dave was over here because I didn't answer?"

"Lie. That's what Jack does. You were on the toilet. You were getting the mail. You were out to dinner with me."

"I'm starting to understand that whole scorned woman thing."

"Don't get mad; get even. Don't you deny yourself happiness because of him. He still goes out and does his thing. He still fucks his wife, probably out of obligation, but he still gets laid. You can too."

I couldn't argue with her. Had I been denying myself happiness? Had I been so swept up in the charade of dominance, power and lust scattered over state lines that I'd lost the concept of what true happiness looked like? One that was free of this one sided convenience?

50

I walk in to the wide open court, hair pulled back into a heavy ponytail, and eyes behind goggles, I hit a few practice rounds, working on my backswing. Dave studies me from outside the court; I pretend not to see his ogling of me through the glass.

"Okay a few things. Your form is getting better, but try planting your feet until you slam the ball. You'll be there in no time." Dave says as he walks in, grabbing me around the waist.

"Yeah, thanks. I think you're a good teacher for me."

"Oh I could teach you some more."

"You could? About what?"

"About what I'd like to do to that stomach of yours, among other things."

Egad. My mind shot to the widespread notion that pilots were notorious womanizers. But I don't think anything could top the mess of man I had been wrapped up in for the past few years.

"Ha, only in your wet dream." I wink at him.

"Oh, haha! You got me there."

"Dave, I've gotta tell you something." I motioned to him with my finger.

"Yeah?" Happiness brewed in his eyes. I didn't want to hurt the guy. But what would be more hurtful was to lead him on, making him believe I was 100% available, in which case, I was not.

"I don't want you to think that this is...going to...progress," I begin, talking with my hands. "I know I had you come over that one time for dinner. And, that infamous shower. And if I perhaps lead you on, I apologize. That was not my intent. I like you. I really do, but I'm not at the right place in my life right now to commit. I enjoy our time together at the gym; you've taught me a lot in racquetball, but I just don't want to get your hopes up for something that will never transpire."

I stop for a moment, looking at him. His face glazed over, taken aback. I couldn't believe the words that had just exited my mouth. I was shooting down my own happiness. Dave I'm sorry I just need time.

"Well, I don't care what you say, I have no regrets. However, I have to respect your decision, as hard as it may be for me to see your beautiful face every time we're in the gym together. I knew you had a boyfriend. A good-looking girl like you doesn't stay single for long."

Now he was jumping to conclusions. Boyfriend?

"No one ever said I had a boyfriend."

"Well, that's what it sounds like."

I roll my eyes. Oh, Dave if you only knew. It's far more complicated than you could ever imagine.

51

November 2013

Summer B had come and gone. Six weeks like a whirlwind. Receiving an A and B in the two classes I'd taken, I was satisfied. As it had been some time since a trip with Jack, the accelerated curriculum had been easier to tackle. That short summer semester was also telling of my and Jack's apparent unraveling. Distance had been heavy these last few weeks. He hadn't stopped by before work in awhile.

My time with him had made me an expert wander-luster, learning things indigenous to New Yorkers, like that 4:30 is shift change and that trying to catch a cab at that time is damn near impossible. All of these little cultural driblets were attributed to him. And all of it, made possible on his philandering coattails.

For a long time, I thought I was happy. It's not that I necessarily needed the trips or the $200 dinners. But I had set my happiness in the lap of someone unavailable. As much as Jack's chicanery had made him seem available, really all of this had been centered around his self-serving attitude. I had become exclusive to a man who wasn't exclusive to me. Sure my phone rang at all hours, early or late, and on all those trips we took I was appalled at the dead phone screen that sat lifeless on the nightstands of hotels across the country. I didn't want a part of his mess anymore.

* * *

*NY trip. Nov. 4-7. 3:25.

I search for that familiar wash of scintillating passion as I read Jack's text. I can't find it. Nothing moved in me. Nothing shook. Instead what filled me was something transient. Something numb. Something that was elusive and selfish all the same. I text him back.

*You know, you're being awfully pushy as usual, for being pretty absent these past few weeks.

*I'm the boss. Don't care.

In typical Jack form, he offset the seriousness of this offense with comedy. I had been nothing but the puppet in this game for far too long. I push around a globule of quinoa with my tongue. My dinner looked less than appealing right now. Pressing it against the roof of my mouth, I hold it there for a second and dump my plate in the trash. My appetite was shot.

Had this been the past, I would have booked that flight by now. It was 6:30 P.M. I would have postponed the gym, phone calls and anything else remotely having to do with myself. I hadn't booked that flight. I didn't even feel a hankering to do so.

* * *

I take myself to the gym for some distraction. Fall was here, my favorite time of the year. I drive past homes whose front doors were adorned with rustic colored wreaths, pumpkins and cornhusks becoming a ubiquitous staple in front yards.

I had lied in my apartment for the past three hours staring up at the ceiling, contemplating my unconventional life. A diorama of sorts played on in my mind where I was a marionette, Jack lurking above with a sinister smile, baiting me with $100 bills. And now, that same marionette clawed at the ceiling, vying for an escape.

* * *

Knife Party sears my eardrums as my subconscious stabs Jack with each glide on the elliptical. It was time for me to get mad. It was time for me to stand up for myself. It was time for me to pursue what was best for Lara, not him.

A tap on the shoulder shook me out of the violent diorama in my mind.

"Oh hey you."

It was Dave.

"What are you doing here?"

"Oh, just wanted to get some cardio in tonight."

"Yeah, like you really need it. You want to hit it around a bit in there?" He motioned to the racquetball courts.

"Sure, why not."

I play the lousiest game of racquetball I've ever done. I miss nearly every shot and my coordination is less than mediocre.

"Hey, you alright? You seem off."

The two of us stand in the middle of the court. His hands on my shoulders, Dave takes one finger and perks my chin up so that my eyes meet his. But I look away. Tears well up. "Sorry, just a rough day. It's nothing really."

"Well surely it is. It's got you upset enough here on the court where you cant even concentrate."

A lump grows in my throat. A warm tingling overtakes my cheeks. *Oh, I want to tell him. I want to tell him about this fucked up state of my life right now but I can't. My very wealthy, very controlling, very domineering, and married boyfriend—the boyfriend that doesn't act married. My boyfriend who gets a streak of jealousy at the mere thought of another infringing on what he claims to be his. Yes, that, is my boyfriend if you want to call it that. The boyfriend who has run my life for the past few years.*

"I'm sorry Dave, I've gotta go."

I take off out of the court.

"Lara. Lara wait!"

52

I wish I could had told Dave everything right then and there. But to try and squeeze my cluster fuck life into a nutshell would prove to be a challenge that I would lose at. I sit at home glazed over my laptop. Another flight, another time, another city. And then a text.

*Make sure you book soon. Don't want prices to go up.

"Fuck off." I mutter aloud to myself.

It was now 10:00 at night. I'd given up long ago wondering how and why he was able to reach out to me at an hour when any other married man would have likely been found in some proverbial familial stance, you know, huddled with the family in front of some cliché TV show.

I hold my head in my hands. The computer screen is stuck on the Delta departures home page to LGA. Tears well up. I move solemnly out to the balcony and gaze down to the lake. The swans are there below, I envy their freedom. I sit in my patio chair, huddled Indian style. I wipe the warm streams from my cheeks.

For too long I had cast aside my frustration with a coy giggle, downplaying what I really felt, all to appease Jack and his demands. Caught in the crossroads of what I wanted and what I'd been conditioned to do for years, once again hit me in the face.

* * *

I decided to play with him. I recalled what Sarah had told me: compartmentalize. What was Jack to me now other than some reduced piece of fodder in which I could mess with? I had six months until I graduated. I wasn't doing this to deliberately hurt Jack. Despite all of his complexities and his jaded charm, the man had helped me immensely. He had footed the bill for much of my college expenses. I felt the carefully molded years of codependence begin to disintegrate from the walls of my mind.

* * *

I text him, borrowing one of his lines.

*Oh NYC? I'm not sure if I can fit you in that particular week.

*Woman, please. You know what happens.

*Oh, won't you remind me?

*Feet pinned by your ears

I recalled how I had acted that initial meeting with Dave. We sat in his car, talking. I nervously checked my phone, anxious for Jack's after work call. I was enjoying that new moment with Dave but also didn't want to upset Jack. And now here I was, throwing that care away so hard and fast, replaced with a newfound apathy for Jack's demands; one I did not know I possessed.

53

I sip my coffee, reading my horoscope. I never took what the readings said to heart, but today's headline particularly resonated with me. "A profound change is on the horizon," and, "You're dealing with repressed feelings that are dying to come out," were just a few recurring themes.

For the first time in my life, the fact that I was actually internalizing what the cosmos was telling me had me questioning the validity of things deemed normative in my life.

* * *

I didn't want to hurt Jack. I just wanted to slip out quietly, undetected. But here I was, once again faced with an opportunity to go out with someone who was actually available—not part-time available—someone who held a genuine interest in me, someone who was just as keen to see me as I was, and yet I had Jack still pushing strong in the background, refusing to be put out.

"Hey. What are you doing?"

"Not much. I was at the gym earlier, just relaxing."

"Book the flight yet?"

I had learned within the first year that the man hated to be refused, and now where I stood was no different from what I'd seen years ago. At the most it was more intense and unwavering. I knew that my behavior would throw a curveball that he was unprepared for. And so I learned from Jack's own tricks. I lied. But trying to tell a lie to a well-practiced liar was no easy feat. And so here I was, assuming that same impassive exterior that he did, explaining that I'd just landed an interview with the *Harbor Observer* at 1:30 Tuesday November 4th, and that I'd be unable to make the flight to NYC.

"So, why don't you just take a later flight out?"

Silence.

"Well, I–"

"What?"

"I actually cancelled it."

"You cancelled the flight? Why?"

I had never cancelled a flight. Ever.

"Well, I don't think you've considered all of what I've got going on." A part of me felt bad for lying to him—lying to a liar. This whole relationship—or what was left of it—was suffocating me.

"This has nothing to do with your interview. The fact that you'd cancel without booking a later flight out is telling."

He was noticeably bitter, pouting for not getting his way, like a child with deep pockets.

54

November 4ᵗʰ was a day full of 'supposed to's'. I was supposed to be on a plane going to New York with Jack. I was supposed to be sitting in the airport, on that all too familiar terminal, with a strategically placed magazine in front of my face. I was supposed to be acting like we were two unassuming strangers. Only I wasn't.

Climbing up to the very top level of the parking deck, I take a spot far away from the assembly of cars. I look at the time. Jack would be here in a mere two hours to fly out to NYC. *What if he sees me? What will I say? Why am I here? He'll catch me in a lie.*

"Hey, where you at?"

Oh my god. My heart palpated in my ears. Anxiety punches me in the gut.

"Hi, I—I'm at the dealership getting my oil changed."

"Oh. I was going to see if I could drop by for a minute before I'm off to NYC." His tone was different from the other day, more solemn.

My heart sank. A cold, hollow feeling filled up my stomach. Words escaped me. It was like he knew I was bullshitting him.

"Oh, well I'm not home right now. Sorry."

"Well can I meet you at the dealership?" "Jack, no—you can't. You know I have so many days that are filled with nothing. Nothing to do, where I am free reign and then you call me when I've got stuff to do."

"Ok, well, just wanted to see you before I went off to New York."

"Well, I'm sorry I didn't wait around at home for you to call. I've got things to do too, you know."

"Well I could stop by just for five minutes and give you some money." "Really? You didn't do that when I went to Seattle. What's the urgency?"

My face grew hot.

"The one time I don't go on a trip with you and this is how you act. I have always, *always* gone with you. Have I *not* revamped my schedule to appease yours for years? And the one time I don't go, you act like a petulant child. It's a bit ridiculous."

My own words echoed in my ears, a sense of power emitting from them, indicative of my newfound rebellion. I had always *had* the time. I had always *made* the time. And now there was a fissure in the order of things. And he didn't like it.

"Alright, well, I guess I'll just go on to the airport then. Sorry." Jack muttered, sounding defeated.

"Ok, well I will see you when you get back. I'm sorry I can't go but you know, you want too much sometimes. It's exhausting. I've gotta go."

"I will back off a bit. Sorry. I think I mistakenly got so consumed in work over the last three months that I've come on too strong lately. I forgot about you and I apologize." Jack apologizing? Who was this man? Grabbing my luggage, I took up light speed into the terminal.

* * *

"Good afternoon, Miss Arbour, where we off to today?"

"New Orleans."

The terminal was abuzz with people. Any other Tuesday I assumed would have looked similar. Fidgeting for my license and credit card, my eyes nervously dart up for any sign of a man about 6'5" and 240.

"The Big Easy," says the curbside checker. "Great town. Great food."

I peer down at the boarding pass. JAX-ATL-MSY. I slight twinge of guilt rose up within me for skipping out on Jack. I quickly slapped it down. *I can do what I want. He's the one that's married. I'm not. I have license to go anywhere, with anybody.*

"Yes, I'll be starting early on the plane."

I shove a crumbled up $5 into the checker's hand and take off.

"Enjoy your trip ma'am!"

I thought about what I wanted. I thought about what I needed. I thought about what I deserved. Half of the problem was that I'd never allowed myself the opportunity for anything better than someone borrowed.

Maneuvering through the mass of briefcases and suits, I bolt to my gate. The time was now 12:25. My flight took off at 1:30, Jack's at 3:25. The chances of him showing up so early were slim. But his hawk-like reflexes wouldn't surprise me if I did bump into him— on the same terminal.

I crouch on the floor between two rows of seats, covering any hint of detail that would give away myself. Gazing at my plane, I whisper for it to begin boarding. *Come on, come on, come on.*

I send a picture of the plane to Dave with a smiley emoji.

*Can't wait to see you. I am in first class but going to switch my seat to sit next to you.

Jack had definitely never pulled that move. I had become so accustomed to being hushed away. This was refreshing.

I remember Jack telling me a long time ago that I didn't exactly blend; that my features made me stick out. And now here I was, trying to blend— and failing miserably at it. And then a text.

*At the airport. It just hit me that this is my third quarterly review in NYC and you're not here. Sucks.

My heart sank. *But no, don't feel guilty. This is not about him anymore it's about you. Oh god. Oh god. He's at the airport.* I looked to the gate information. Fifteen minutes until boarding. A very *long* fifteen minutes. I was taking

281

Delta as was Jack, he'd always taken Delta to NYC. I looked to the neighboring gate information. *Shit.*

"3:25 LaGuardia."

Oh man. What are the fucking chances that my gate is right next to Jack's? *How was I going to leave here? How was I going to hop on that plane to Atlanta? How was I going to skip by without him seeing me? Oh my god, what the fuck am I going to say if he sees me?*

I'd been just as guilty as he in creating this hidden life. And while it had been a hell of a ride, that clandestine dream was beginning to slip between my fingers, and I wasn't scampering to pick up the pieces.

Now I was faced with a new dichotomy, one that didn't include running with someone under the radar. Sparked by the taste of something obtainable, something I could really embrace and not just hold to for a little while and let go. I pull out my phone and began to text him back.

*I'm sorry I am not there, but I've always been. Have I not rearranged my schedule, skipped classes and rushed off at a moment's notice all to appease you? I have.

*I know I've fucked up. This is why you're not here. Those words pulsated at me like a light in the dark. I'd never heard him mutter anything remotely hinting to a sense of emotion—and definitely not in such a melancholy manner.

*Fucked up how?

*Because you're not here. Not your fault.

Oh my god. Was this Jack cowering down before me?
The shell of a man so tightly confined seemingly began
to shatter. A man I had always known as impassive and
lacking a moral compass began to emit something that
resembled feeling—something so inherently human.

I stretch my legs out from the tightly wound Indian-style
pose I've held for the past forty-five minutes. I dart my
head out above the rows. No sign of him. Standing up, I
brush myself off and affix myself to the nearest column.
Scanning the corridor, for the first time, I legitimately
felt scared of Jack. But why? What was this impromptu
pang of guilt and fear? What had I to feel guilty about?
Jack's incessant demands over the years had crippled my
independent shell, replacing it with a dilapidated sense
of self.

* * *

Buzz.

I text him Jack back a sad Emoji.

*Not your fault. I'm the one sitting in the back of this terminal restaurant with tears.

Oh shit. He's in the terminal? Oh my god. My eyes scan the lobby over rows of travelers. One was methodically combed, parted to one side, hunched over a laptop at a restaurant bar. It was Jack.

"Holy sh—" I mutter under my breath, trembling behind the column. By some sort of divine intervention or incredible stroke of luck, Jack had by the will of the universe, sat with his back to the boarding area. The only challenge left would be to board this plane without him spotting me. Fuck.

"Delta airlines flight # 3417 to Atlanta, we will begin boarding in five minutes."

Glued to the column, I periodically stick my head out to check on Jack. Still huddled over his laptop, back to me. How did it get this way? Two people once so intertwined, intoxicated by the other, now adrift. But then I thought to her: how did that union ever get to its current state of being royally fucked up?

What if I get caught? *Why am I worried about getting caught? Who is he? He's no one. Go, you are not barred to anyone. You are a free woman. Go get what you deserve. But I am hurting him, I don't want to hurt him. Look at all the times he's hurt you. Forget the money, forget the trips, it was all to benefit him, don't you see?* I need a drink.

"Business class and disabled passengers are free to board at this time to Atlanta, Georgia." Was this a full flight? Well I wasn't surprised. Atlanta was a hoppin' airport.

*Can't believe you're not here.

A part of me grinned with satisfaction.

"Economy class passengers, group B now boarding to Atlanta, Georgia."

I cut in front of a mother with two squabbling toddlers, looking over my shoulder to Jack. I didn't see the top of his head. Where was he? I stepped up to the gate agent, my ticket sticking to my damp palms.

"Well, look at that, it doesn't want to let go of you! Thank you, enjoy your flight Miss Arbour." *Yes, shut the fuck up and let me get on this plane.*

I scramble onto the jet bridge. A text from Jack.

"Funny, I just saw your twin at the airport here. "

55

I take my seat. I can't believe I just did that. Holy fuck.

"Anything to drink ma'am?"

"Yes, a cabernet please."

Sure it was the afternoon. And I had never had a drink on all those flights with Jack. But today, after the stunt I'd just pulled, it was definitely warranted.

I look out the window as we ascend through the clouds. Was this really happening? Tears welled up in my eyes. I felt more conflicted than ever before, in a kind of purgatory where feelings of guilt and freedom tugged at me. *Oh my god, I think he saw me. Shit.*

Maybe I hadn't realized how truly bad Jack was

for me until recently. Perhaps the trips, dinners, and money had clouded my vision for a good number of years. For the first time in our lengthy existence, I rejected him. The man became revolting, an effigy for something spineless. Impassive. Selfish. Overwhelming. Energy sucking—the true underbelly of sociopathic tendencies.

That half smile that had once crept across my face with each phone call had now been replaced with a loathsome sense of a chore—of something I had to do— pick up the phone, nod agreeably, rearrange my schedule to appease his, you know the drill. You also know it gets worse if you don't pick up the phone.

* * *

I arrive in Hartsfield-Atlanta airport one hour later. My phone is riddled with texts from Jack.

*Text you when I land in NYC. Miss you.

*Can't believe you're not with me.

I'll admit his sorrowful demeanor made me twirl inside. A kind of power struggle that had gone on for years suddenly was flipped in my favor. I relished in it. I step off the train onto Concourse C and meet Dave.

"Hey you."

Smiling, I embrace him hard and kiss him on the cheek. Dressed in pilot apparel, he looked scrumptious. This was his last stop for the day. Instead of going home to Marsh Harbor, we had decided on an impromptu trip to New Orleans.

"I can't believe Marsh Harbor doesn't have a direct to New Orleans."

"I know, Atlanta is a bigger airport, they service more destinations. That's why I flew you up here. You look great."

I bat my lashes at him. He didn't know the extent of what I had left behind, or the years of anguish and mental conditioning that I had gotten swept up in. I wasn't sure if I'd ever tell him. Some things were better left as quiet triumphs.

Boarding the plane, we take a seat in first class, Dave sitting beside me. An innocuous move like this had me reeling.

* * *

Dave and I sit at the Carousel Bar inside the Hotel
Monteleone. Outside, pedestrians mosey along, drinks
in hand. There's a kind of stench that emanates from the
streets, evocative of revelers partying hardy: dried
whisky, urine and other bad decisions. Arbitrary strands
of beads hang from the power lines. A palm reader
motions for tourists to come and get their future
revealed. A drifter plays a cover of Louis Armstrong's
version of "La vie en Rose" on a violin, tourists toss
dollar bills into his instrument case as they pass
by. "This must be why it's dubbed the big easy. I've
never seen a place where you can carry an open
container."

"Yeah, New Orleans is its own kind of beast." The
Monteleone was one of the oldest in New Orleans, a
Royal Street staple since the late 1800's. A jazz quartet
croons a cover of Louis Prima's "Just a gigolo" in the
corner, and I look at the reflection of Dave and I from
the mirrors and jester busts that stare down at us from
the bar.

"Have you ever tried a Sazerac? It's indigenous to New
Orleans." Dave asks, pushing it in front of me.

"No I haven't."

I take a sip of it, my face pruning.

"Oh my god! That's putrid!"

"I'm happy you're here. You look quite different out of those gym clothes."

Dave scans the green shift dress I'd donned for the evening. Tan strappy stilettos however, proved to be a fashion faux pas here in this city. The streets of the French Quarter were permanently disfigured from years of hurricanes, most notably Katrina. The potholes and nooks and crannies were anything but friendly to a beautiful pair of heels.

"So how is it possible you've been single for as long as you have been? I mean, you've got the looks, the confidence, and the education. Hell, maybe you are too much for some guys."

I take a sip of my wine and reflect on what he'd just said. Confidence. An attribute that had always been inherent had become something that I had to relinquish back. My years with Jack had almost kidnapped that self-assured confidence that is a byproduct of independence.

"Yeah, I suppose so. The one thing I won't ever be is some docile female that men can walk all over."

"That's the exact thing I admire about you. Too many people get wrapped up in inhibitions, afraid to say what they mean, and mean what they say. That's how that gray area happens in relationships. And then from that gray area comes a rift in communication. Then the sex fades. You become housemates. That's how divorces ensue."

An imaginary sequence of Jack's less than ideal marital bliss plays out in my head. I recall Jack telling me the numerous times he'd show up late after work due to a meeting or some gallivant with me; coming home to a plate sitting in the microwave and sitting solo at a dining room table that only three ever sat at.

If anything, I was free of the pain. I was free of the deceit. I had witnessed firsthand the manipulated synergy of Jack. Like him, I had compartmentalized his position in my life. I no longer looked at him through an enigmatic haze but more so a pragmatic scope. Over the years, my time with him had me question convictions of happiness, the fundamental needs of humans, and that façade of normalcy that many marriages strive to attain when they're beyond broken.

Dave kisses me on the cheek and grabbing me by the hand, we go out to explore the Quarter. For once in my life, I was unbothered with being in the right place to receive Jack's texts. Perhaps unfettered was a more fitting word.

56

2014

I sit with Jack in the same restaurant I had taken a seat in nearly four years earlier. The same place where I had once scribbled down my monthly expenses, opening myself to years of dominance clouded by the bait of financial security. I struggled to find a moniker for myself while in New Orleans. The one that fit was that I had indeed been a kept woman, to no one's fault but my own. I didn't look at Jack with disdain but more so pity, for he was the true loser in this game; a conflicted, selfish mess of a man fueled by zeal for things that spelled a challenge; one that money had ruined. I had been nothing but a pretty accessory to his charade of power.

"Jack, you're talking to the girl that told you from the

get-go I didn't want money. You were the one that sent envelopes in the mail. You were the one who made me list my expenses. You were the one who willingly footed the bill for my tuition and living expenses. I never asked for any of this."

Hanging his head low, he grabs my hand, intertwining his fingers with mine. I hadn't seen him in one year.

"You've helped me immensely but I've never let anyone else in because I knew you wouldn't like it. You wanted me to be available to you, and if I dated someone that would put that in jeopardy."

"I see. Well, do what you have to do. Come for one last dance. Have to do a steak and wine, end it like it began."

He was going to New York on business again, and was failing miserably at trying to get me to tag along. I couldn't believe he was still trying after I'd just technically broke this off. Well he hated to lose.

"Jack, no. I can't. Not anymore."

"I see. Let me think. Going to have some fun playing in the second position."

"What's that supposed to mean?"

"I am in second position to your new guy. It's fun

actually."

"And I never was to your wife? I mean, thank god I was on this side of it and not living with blinders like she apparently is."   I sit, my mind in a state of paralysis. If this wasn't the pot calling the kettle black I didn't know what was. It was like he totally disregarded the fact that he was married—and jealous at that.

"If that's how you feel, then the thing failed."

"What? What thing?"

"My entire goal was to make you happy and successful. I always found you too intelligent for that atmosphere where we met. I provided for you so that you could focus your energies on studying, not how many dances you could rack up in a night. The goal was to get a girl out of the strip club, graduated, and onto better things."

While I heard what he was saying, I also did not let myself forget the years of control and dominance that had come with this assistance. The double standards. The convenience factor. The his way or the highway. All of it. Had it been worth it?

"I feel like I'm crazy. I meet girls in clubs that shouldn't be there, and I cannot help."

I look at him. This was a new Jack that I hadn't seen in those four years. One that exuded empathy, something unknown to the one I had fallen for and shared countless adventures with. The Jack I had known was impassive and austere, one that repressed emotion like a pro.

"You did help. You helped me get through college. I graduated. I am no longer in that atmosphere that I met you in. But you—you are the one who needs help—you thrive on vice and at the expense of others' feelings. You do not care who you hurt in the process of getting what you want."

"You know me better than most."

"I know the side you keep hidden from everyone— fellow parents at the kids' games, your colleagues, hell, even your wife. I mean doesn't this kind of hiding around get old after awhile Jack? The two phones, the toting of gym bags when you're not really going to the gym…all of it."

"Maybe I'm not ready to stop."

Cold, methodical and expressionless: a throwback to my Jack. The Jack I had known. I wondered how much longer he'd remain in a sad state of stagnation with the buffer of a big home that muffles the tension. Something barked in me to get up and leave. The pain was replaced by a cut and dry slice of reality.

"I am not a good person."

"I know. But she doesn't."

* * *

August of 2014 I walked away from the Coastal College of Florida a newly minted graduate with a Bachelor's in English. I shook hands, gave hugs and posed for photos. There were graduation gifts and copious amounts of glowing praise. I was the second on my dad's side to graduate college and the first on my mom's. It was an enigmatic day. But as I walked across that stage to receive my degree, there was one face that I wished could had been there. A solemn thought rang out to the one man who had kept me afloat through all those years, at the sacrifice of my own happy endeavors beyond his zealous demands. But you could never expect much from a man like Jack.

That day when I left the restaurant, I saw a glimpse of a luggage ID tag with an address. It must have fallen out of his pocket when he left for the bathroom. All this time, I never knew where he lived. He had been so good at covering his tracks. I followed it back home. Low and behold, it was a mere ten miles from my apartment. Walking up to the door of a sprawling abode that had once danced in my imagination, I rang the doorbell and dumped years of plane tickets, hotel receipts and a key card bearing his last name. A woman opened the door as I drove away. I smiled.

Perhaps an old Katharine Hepburn sums it up best, "Sometimes I wonder if men and women really suit each other. Perhaps they should live next door and just visit now and then."

ABOUT THE AUTHOR

Camille Lindstrom is a graduate of the University of North Florida, where she earned a BA English. This is her first book.

Made in the USA
Charleston, SC
24 December 2016